BLACKWORK

BLACKWORK

MONICA FERRIS

THORNDIKE
CHIVERS

This Large Print edition is published by Thorndike Press, Waterville, Maine, USA and by AudioGO Ltd, Bath, England.

Thorndike Press, a part of Gale, Cengage Learning.

A Needlecraft Mystery.

The text of this Large Print edition is unabridged.

Other aspects of the book may vary from the original edition.

Set in 16 pt. Plantin.

Printed on permanent paper.

LIBRARY OF CONGRESS CATALOGING-IN-PUBLICATION DATA

Ferris, Monica.
    Blackwork / by Monica Ferris.
      p. cm. — (Thorndike Press large print mystery)
    ISBN-13: 978-1-4104-2316-0 (alk. paper)
    ISBN-10: 1-4104-2316-6 (alk. paper)
    1. Devonshire, Betsy (Fictitious character)—Fiction. 2. Needleworkers—Fiction. 3. Women detectives—Fiction. 4. Halloween—Fiction. 5. Minnesota—Fiction. 6. Large type books. I. Title.
    PS3566.U47B57 2010
    813'.54—dc22
                                   2009045816

BRITISH LIBRARY CATALOGUING-IN-PUBLICATION DATA AVAILABLE

Published in 2010 in the U.S. by arrangement with The Berkley Publishing Group, a member of Penguin Group (USA) Inc.

Published in 2010 in the U.K. by arrangement with the author.

U.K. Hardcover: 978 1 408 47832 5 (Chivers Large Print)
U.K. Softcover: 978 1 408 47833 2 (Camden Large Print)

Printed and bound in Great Britain by
CPI Antony Rowe, Chippenham, Wiltshire
1 2 3 4 5 6 7 14 13 12 11 10 09

ACKNOWLEDGMENTS

Mark Pasquinelli, Blake Richardson (the owner of Herkimer's Microbrewery), and the brewmasters at Granite City in St. Louis Park, Minnesota, taught me about beer making. Fiona MacGregor and Ann Peters helped me learn about Wicca (and Betty Noel, too). Dr. Robert Sherman helped me with some technical details. The song sung by Leona Cunningham is "Savage Daughter," by SCA bard Wyndreth Berginsdottir, aka Karen Kahan. I thank Alix Jordan for creating and naming Conner Sullivan. And thanks to Kreinik Manufacturing for the beautiful, appropriate pattern in the back of this book.

And particular thanks is given to my wonderful editor, the bestseller-maker Jackie Cantor; my agent, the bargain-broker Nancy Yost; Berkley Prime Crime's art director George Long, and the illustrator Mary Ann Lasher, who together come up with my beautiful covers; and my informal editor, the one who keeps me from sending a manuscript off to New York full of bloomers, Ellen Kuhfeld.

PROLOGUE

Leona Cunningham hovered over a medium-size black cauldron suspended from a tripod above a fire in her backyard. She was a slim woman, a little taller than average. Her long dark hair, well streaked with silver, was pulled back in a careless knot. She was dressed all in black: black sweater, black jeans, black boots. It was early evening, and the sun was so low that its beams came through a thick stand of trees at the back of her lot. In the low-angled light, the flames of her fire were more felt than seen, casting a warm aura across the beaten earth that surrounded the fire pit. The warmth was welcome; it had been a chilly fall day, with deeply gray skies that had broken open only a few minutes ago.

The weather had started turning cool in late summer. If the signs were right, it was going to be a chilly, wet fall that would turn into a cold, snowy winter.

Leona Cunningham knew how to interpret the signs because she was a witch. She had practiced Wicca, the New Age form of a very old earth-worshipping religion, for decades. One of her gifts in Wicca was understanding the weather. She was rarely wrong in predicting a season.

She stirred the mixture in the pot, which was giving off a fragrance like hot cereal. This wasn't surprising — it was a mash consisting of ground roasted barley and water, a prelude to beer. Leona pulled some of the burning wood away from the cauldron so it wouldn't boil. She'd been doing this for so many years she didn't need a thermometer to know how hot the mash was. Still . . . "Double, double, don't cause trouble, fire burn, but mash don't bubble," muttered Leona, stirring some more. She tried a cackle, but it was a failure. "Darn it, I just can't get that ratchety sound no matter how I try," she lamented to herself as she broke into a genuine chuckle.

Moving skillfully, she lifted the cauldron off the fire, poured its contents through a big strainer into another cauldron, then put the liquid on the fire. Murmuring a charm, she tossed in a measure of dried hops to cut the sweetness. She added wood chips to the fire to bring the liquid, now called *wort,* to a swift, rolling boil, then stepped back to fan her brow with the hot pad. It being autumn in Minnesota, dusk had turned to night with the swiftness of a closing trap door, so now the red and yellow flames were brightly visible.

In the chill of the night, Leona's face cooled quickly. She went up to her back porch and turned on a bright light, then returned to look at the boiling cauldron and stir some more. It wasn't really smart to do serious brewing over an open fire; she should be using propane. But Leona was a traditionalist — a real traditionalist, reaching back centuries for her methods.

For the next hour, between stirring the wort and adjusting the fire — boiling was good, boiling over was disaster — she sat on the top step and let her mind ramble.

Leona was the senior partner in Excelsior's microbrewery-pub, The Barleywine. Thirty years earlier, it had begun as the Waterfront Café. She and her late husband, John, had founded and operated it. After his death three years ago, she kept it open, but slowly added items to the menu — herbed potato salad, soy bread wraps, and flavored teas — to augment the tuna melts and french fries some customers still demanded. Most of the recipes were her own creations, and the herbs came from her own garden.

Two years ago the little beauty shop next to the café went out of business and Leona bought the building. She started a second business, Natural Solutions, selling herbal soaps, candles, shampoos, and cooking ingredients. But she was soon overwhelmed by the amount of time it took to make the many little products, time taken from the established business of her restaurant. She couldn't afford to hire a company to make the herbal products for her, wouldn't buy artificial ingredients, and buying natural products to sell seemed a duplication of effort. She began to think that acquiring the building had been a mistake.

Then a friend complimented her on a potion she had made. Not a tea, not a medicine, but beer. Leona's husband had made beer — he'd learned how from his grandfather, who had made it during prohibition. Leona had been surprised at how easy it was, and how natural. Like her other herbal preparations, there was nothing artificial in it. Barley, water, yeast, and hops formed the basic recipe. Her friend said Leona's brews tasted even better than her husband's had.

So she continued to experiment with the

many varieties of hops and yeasts, the occasional sugar or herbal flavoring, and brewing at higher and lower temperatures, until she had four or five different brews that were really, really good. Two had won blue ribbons at the Minnesota State Fair.

When Leona found out a microbrewery in Saint Paul was closing and the equipment was to be offered at auction, she went over for a look at it. It was good-quality stuff, well cared for. She put in what she was sure was a too-low bid — and won.

Then she went to cash in some investments to pay for the remodeling of the herb shop — only to discover that most of the money had gone missing. From the holes in his story, she theorized that her dishonest investment counselor had taken it to cover some earlier thefts.

Leona had already mortgaged her house to transform Curl Up & Dye into Natural Solutions, and she feared that she would lose everything — until a friend, Billie Leslie, came forward with a proposal. Billie had experience in restaurant management and wanted to try ownership. For a share in Leona's place, she would contribute an amount equal to the purloined funds. After a short hesitation, Leona agreed.

Although as a rule she didn't like sharing,

Leona was pleased to find that Billie worked just as hard as she did in The Barleywine, and at present that work was paying for itself. Still, it would have been nice to be sole proprietor, to make all the decisions herself — and quickly. Billie took forever to make up her mind about things.

Why couldn't I have stayed with herbals, like a good, traditional witch? she asked herself as she sat on her back porch, watching the clouds close in again and feeling a fresh breeze spring up. But she knew the answer to that. From an early age she had marched to the beat of a different drummer. Her parents, good Lutherans, had been amused at first, then bemused, then disappointed in their younger daughter. So had Leona's elder sister, Judy. It had taken Judy years to come around, but her parents never did. Leona's daughter, Willow, practiced Wicca, but very subtly. Good thing Willow's husband was agnostic. It would be interesting to see what beliefs they transmitted to their children when — if — they ever had any.

Meanwhile, she would continue brewing beer. For one thing, it was organic. And it was old, old, old. The earliest example of writing, a clay cuneiform tablet, proved to be a Sumerian inventory of warehoused beer. The ancient Egyptians, on break from

12

building pyramids, drank beer.

Beer and wine were safer than untreated water, knowledge people treasured down the centuries.

Benjamin Franklin said that beer is proof that God loves us and wants us to be happy. Leona had done a counted cross-stitch of that motto and hung it up at The Barley-wine, even though she didn't believe in the God old Ben was talking about.

One good thing about having a partner in business was that Leona occasionally had time to indulge another one of her passions: needlework. She directed a mental blessing at Betsy Devonshire and her shop, Crewel World. Nice to have it local, well run, and well stocked with lots of counted cross-stitch patterns.

Too bad poor Betsy thought she had to spend Sunday morning in church, praying that her shop continued to do well. All owners of small businesses — Leona included — often walked in unsafe proximity to bankruptcy.

But Leona liked Wicca because it wasn't a petitionary religion. The Christians and Jews were encouraged to ask their God for favors. In Leona's mind, this put them in the position of children — and Leona had resented being treated like a child even when she was one. Wicca maintained that people had power within themselves; they just had to learn how to plug into it. It had taken years, and there had been and still were failures. But when it worked, it was like riding Pegasus, soaring upward on the wings of that power. A few falls had taught Leona to go carefully, wisely, and to build shields against the unexpected.

She was amazed by atheists, even more so than by Christians. Didn't they see how *alive* the world was? How full of invisible influences? She checked her watch, rose and went into the house, and came back with two big bags of ice cubes. She sliced the bags open with a pocket knife and poured the ice into her biggest cauldron.

After giving the boiling cauldron a final stir, Leona unhooked it from the tripod and set it with a loud hiss into the icy cauldron, stirring and stirring to make sure it cooled quickly and evenly. She dipped into it with a quart-size glass pitcher and set that aside on a flat rock.

Then she cleared her mind of residual angry or resentful thoughts about Billie Leslie, her perforce partner. And while she was at it, her anger at Ryan McMurphy, who while sober was a fine, upstanding citizen but while drunk, a disgusting and angry bigot. It could spoil the brew to make it while unhappy; and to allow angry or unhappy thoughts to take up residence could lead to thoughts of hexes and curses. That way madness lay.

When her mind was sweet and calm, she recited a brief charm to bless the living yeast and added it to the pitcher, stirred thoroughly, then added it to the cooled cauldron, stirring and stirring. The yeast would eat the sugar released by boiling the grain, turning it into alcohol. She had put in just enough hops to give it the familiar bitterness of beer — American beers, in her opinion, were generally overhopped — and now added a little anise for exotic flavor.

She siphoned the wort — there were about three gallons — into a big glass jug and put an airlock on it that would allow gasses to escape while preventing outside air from slipping in to contaminate the brew.

If she liked the dark ale that resulted, she would make a full-size batch in her microbrewery at The Barleywine. She turned the yard light off and just stood awhile, looking up at the dark sky. Ancient peoples had been afraid of the dark; modern peoples drove it away with streetlights and lamps. But Leona had never been afraid of the dark. In her mind's eye she could see the big glass jug sitting on the earth, the earth turning toward the darkness as the yeast began its stealthy work.

She would call it Don't Be Afraid of the Dark Ale.

ONE

It was a dark, blustery afternoon.

In October an occasional raw day was expected, sometimes even welcome after a hot, dry summer. But it had been a cool summer, and now it was a dark, wet, cold autumn. Godwin had turned on every light in the shop to keep the depressing outdoors at bay, but it pressed against the big front window, dimming the bright colors of the knitting yarns on display. A different kind of rainy autumn — with rackety thunderstorms that left the air sharp and clean and shiny — wouldn't have been so miserable. But since mid-September, the days had grown short and gloomy, with chilly rain dripping from clouds that rarely parted to let the sun shine in.

Like today. Thin streamers of water dribbled down the big front window of Crewel World like the tears of a child whose dog has died.

Godwin sat down at the big library table, on a chair that faced the well-lit back, away from the tears. He picked up a piece of cross-stitch he'd been working on, a Mike Vickery chart of three brilliant Amazon macaws sitting in tropical foliage. He was stitching it on fourteen-count linen in the brightest colors DMC offered. Betsy wasn't there, so he'd put a Jimmy Buffet album in the CD player — Betsy allowed only soft jazz or classical when she was in the shop — and was nodding in agreement while Jimmy sang about winding up in some tropical bay and wailed, "You need a holllllllliday!"

The door made its two-note announcement that someone was coming in. Godwin put down his stitching and hopped up to greet her — the shop sold needlework and needlework supplies, so naturally most of its customers were women.

Only this time it wasn't. A slim young man stood just inside the door shaking water off his stylish gray fedora. He was dark, a little over Godwin's height — Godwin was five seven — an extraordinarily handsome Spaniard, with thick black hair and bright brown eyes. Even his smile was handsome.

"Rafael!" exclaimed Godwin. "What brings you out in this weather? Not that I'm not happy to see you!" He reached to take the man's hand but was drawn instead into an embrace.

"*¡Mi amigo!*" said Rafael with a chuckle.

"Oh, hey, you're all wet!" protested Godwin, anxious about his brown and green alpaca sweater.

"So I have been told on occasion," said Rafael in the slightly formal tone that came so naturally to him. He released Godwin and stepped back.

Godwin looked up to see if his friend was really hurt, and saw a warm smile. He continued looking, now to admire Rafael's clothing.

His gray wool overcoat with the tie belt was a perfect match in color for the fedora. Around his neck he wore a gold-colored, loosely knit scarf so enormous it was practically a shawl. With all this, plus his narrow trousers and thin black shoes, he looked like an illustration in an upscale magazine article entitled, "What the Fashionable Man Is Wearing."

"Are you not glad to see me?" he asked, the smile starting to fade.

Godwin's heart turned over. "Oh, Rafael," he sighed, and turned away so the man would not glimpse the hope shining in his eyes. Godwin had been disappointed a few times this past summer, and by incipient partners far less worthy than this one.

When he got his emotions under control, he turned back. "What brings you to the shop?"

"My condo was feeling too small, so I decided to be brave about the weather. And anyway, I wanted to see you in your own setting." He looked around, nodding in approval.

Godwin had mentioned he would like Rafael to come to Crewel World to see him "in his natural setting," but also to have Betsy meet him.

Not that Godwin needed Betsy's approval of Rafael, of course. But Godwin's susceptible heart had led him into some situations he quickly regretted, and he felt he needed a backup opinion on this new interest.

"I want also to meet the woman who is your boss," said Rafael, and at this seeming reading of his mind, Godwin's eyebrows lifted in surprise.

Rafael had a beautiful laugh, deep and rich and whole-hearted. "You want me to meet her, too!" he said, pleased to have guessed. Godwin laughed with him. No one who laughed like that could be a bad person. He was sure Betsy would agree.

Godwin had thought of introducing some

of his friends to Rafael and later seeking their opinion. He had decided not to, sure that if they met Rafael, they'd either bad-mouth him or try to woo him away.

So now here was Rafael, ready to be anatomized. Godwin, a lover of language, had come across the word *anatomized* in an old book, and had looked it up and discovered that it meant to analyze in great detail. But what if Betsy didn't approve? Worse, what if she perceived something awful about him?

Well, what if she did? Was her opinion likely to be good in the first place? After all, Betsy had her own unhappy history with men.

Rafael had walked away to look around the shop while Godwin was turning these things over in his mind. They'd rearranged the shop recently, and now the shallow front section, marked off by the antique, white-painted counter, was devoted entirely to knitting yarns, needles, patterns, and supplies. Counted cross-stitch patterns, fabrics, floss, and other materials took up the biggest area in the center; and needlepoint canvases, wools, needles, and other supplies were stored in the back, behind a half wall of box shelves. The walls in the central area were covered with framed models of cross-stitch patterns. Some were small and beautiful; some were large, complex, and beautiful; some were amusing or clever. There were alphabet samplers, witches and jack-o'-lanterns, animals, seascapes, flags and eagles, teapots, English cottages, comic Santas, farmyards, elaborately gowned women, to name just a few. Most were done in counted cross-stitch, but some showcased other kinds of needlework, such as bargello, candlewick, or Hardanger. Rafael walked around, as absorbed as if he were in a museum.

Godwin let him wander. At last Rafael returned to say, "And this, *this,* is your 'fun little hobby'?" He flung a hand up and outward. "How dare you speak of it so slightingly! Many of these things are very beautiful, and doubtless they are very difficult to execute! No wonder your heart is so blithe, when you work among such beautiful things all day long! Your boss must be an amazing woman, so — so charming, so artistic, and then to turn so *feminine* an occupation into a *business!* I want to meet her! Where is she?"

"She's at a meeting. The whole city of Excelsior is going to hold a big Halloween celebration in a few weeks, with a parade and everything, and she's on the planning committee for the parade."

"Oh, yes, you told me of that event. And she is helping with it? She is a woman of many talents, I see."

"Oh, yes, more than you know — more than *I* know, probably. I worry about her sometimes. I mean, she's already got the hassle of this shop plus she owns the building — or will in about four hundred more mortgage payments — so why she takes on more grief is a puzzle to me."

"You think planning a parade in a small town is a big grief?"

Godwin smiled sourly. "You have no idea."

The main problem was that the organizing committee for the fall festival was too big. Not many hands making light work, but too many chefs spoiling the broth. Fourteen chefs to be exact, almost every one of them insisting his or her opinion be heard.

Billie Leslie had never organized anything bigger than a church picnic, but she had a solid, authoritarian manner that made people frequently turn to her for guidance. On the other hand, she was slow to cut off discussions, even when things were getting bogged down in talk.

Decisions had taken too long from the start. What kind of autumn festival was it going to be? A Halloween celebration? A mini–Macy's Thanksgiving Parade? How about the ultimate in nonoffensive, politically correct events, a celebration of the pretty-colored leaves?

The "pretty-colored leaves" supporters were quickly defeated, but it wasn't until after the third planning meeting that the leader of the Thanksgiving contingent discovered she had to go to Pennsylvania for a son's sudden marriage, which gave the Halloween contingent their chance to rally and win.

The meeting to decide the specifics of the Halloween festival was particularly rancorous. Some wanted a parade. Others wanted the sidewalks lined with booths. Some wanted games and dancing on the common by the lake. Someone suggested a huge cookout, others felt families would enjoy individual post-summer picnics, and still others wanted hot dog stands, that fellow who sold pork chops on a stick, and the woman who made fabulous fruit smoothies. Everyone had an opinion and was willing to share it, at length, with the committee. And what was to happen if it rained — or snowed? Snow was not unknown in autumn in Excelsior. Normally there were at least flurries by Halloween. Billie's solution was to set up subcommittees to work problems out. Eventually, there were eleven subcommittees, some with as few as one member.

At a meeting that ran two hours past its scheduled end, there was a compromise of sorts. They'd have it all: pork chops, a picnic, a pickup tag football game, and booths on the common; three — three! — costume contests (children from infants to age six, children from seven to fourteen, and adults), booths on the sidewalks, two bands, *and* a parade. Someone suggested a torchlight parade, pointing out that since the floats and costumes were to be done by amateurs, dim lighting could only help. At least ten people insisted on making a statement of agreement to that last suggestion.

That was the last meeting Betsy had attended. She wouldn't have gotten involved in the first place, except that Billie was a good customer at Crewel World so Betsy saw her often — and she'd proved vulnerable to Billie's blandishments. But Betsy was glad to be the sole member of her committee, and relieved that her assignment was simple. She was to set the order of the units in the parade, and to be there on the night in question to make sure they set off in that order. Since she didn't get to choose the "units," and since the final list would not be available until near the date of the event, she couldn't see how her attendance was helpful, much less essential at the big meetings. So every other week she sent a letter saying that planning on the parade order was coming along nicely, and assumed that her report was read into the minutes.

Then a letter arrived, one sent to all members: The second-to-last meeting was mandatory, as the entire event's planning would be brought under review and finalized. Because Billie had to work, the meeting would take place at The Barleywine.

Betsy told Godwin that she had to leave work at three, but hoped to be back in time to help close up at five. "Where's the meeting?" he asked.

"The Barleywine. Billie can't get away."

"Oh? Well, maybe drinks will be served. Try the stout. It's strong but good."

Actually, Betsy thought there might be a little celebratory drinking. The planning was done. This was simply a review, Billie had assured everyone, to make sure each person's assignment was complete, that nothing had been forgotten, and everyone knew what he or she was responsible for.

Rainy and chill as it was outside, Betsy nevertheless elected to walk to The Barleywine. It was only a couple of blocks up Lake

Street, then not even a block up Water.

Not that long ago, it had been the Water-front Café, and Betsy still felt a nostalgic sense of loss that the old-fashioned restaurant was gone. She was glad the current owners were still offering some of the original country café entrées. Sometimes the taste buds insisted on an old-fashioned hot turkey sandwich awash in gravy.

Betsy lowered her umbrella and ducked into the pub. The interior hadn't been changed a whole lot. There were still two booths in the back, and small square tables in the main seating area, though now each was ornamented by a big pottery beer stein, the kind with a pewter lid. But where there had been a hardwood floor, there was rough-cut slate; and the lunch counter was now a bar, one of those massive freestanding antique ones with carved corners and a brass rail. There was a young man behind the bar, polishing glasses. Behind him was a clear glass wall, through which the micro-brewery setup could be seen.

It looked like a factory or a laboratory in there, with three big stainless steel kettles and four tall tanks, an even bigger tank shaped like a silo, and a control panel with red and green lights. Leona was amid all the equipment, wearing rubber boots and thick rubber gloves, feeding a fat tan hose into one of the kettles.

"Here you are!" said a voice, and Betsy turned to see Billie Leslie offering her a sheet of paper. She was a short, slender person, but vibrant and cheerful. "Here's the agenda!"

Betsy took it and her heart sank. The sheet was covered with small type, top to bottom, single-spaced, with lots of bullets. Surely D-Day didn't take this much planning. And Billie didn't even look apologetic, Betsy noted resentfully.

Betsy was the last arrival. Now all fourteen planners were present — plus a nonmember, a man Betsy recognized as her auto mechanic, Ryan McMurphy. But he was seated off by himself in one of the booths, lingering thoughtfully over a soft drink.

Billie, clearly anxious to get started, gestured at Betsy to find an empty chair. Then she came herself to stand at the head of the tables.

Billie's real first name was Wilhemina — she was named after her great-grandmother — but anyone who called her that was liable to get a look so cold icicles would form on his earlobes. She was in her late forties, with graying auburn hair plaited into a pair of thick braids pinned up on her head. Her hair was very fine and determinedly curly, pulling out of its confinement to form a kind of mist around her head. She wore The Barleywine uniform of a dark-blue T-shirt and trousers, under a linen-colored apron two sizes too big for her. She had a strong, straight nose, electric blue eyes under level brows, and a wide, thin mouth bracketed by deep lines and weighted down at the corners by life's hard lessons.

Billie took a seat herself and looked around the table with that mouth and those eyes, and mutiny at the long agenda died aborning.

Finally, thought Betsy. *She's going to assert her authority.*

But alas. First came Old Business. The finance subcommittee reported that sales of ads in the souvenir program had finally increased enough to cover the printer's charges. Two other members expressed satisfaction at the news, while another wanted to know if the fees were tax-free and started the one lawyer on the committee off on a long exposition on nonprofits and city events. Finally, another committee member cut him off with, "Can we *please* stick to business?"

The head of the food committee reported at length about the two people who would be selling fresh popcorn, and about the candy apple vendor, the pork chop setup, and the hot dog stand.

The security committee presented the very tall, fair-haired Sergeant Lars Larson of the Excelsior Police Department, who announced that Excelsior PD was going to ask for assistance from other jurisdictions and that there might be as many as a dozen sworn peace officers in attendance. Or as few as eight, depending on what else was going on. Billie cut off a discussion about whether or not to ask the Hennepin County Sheriff's Department for assistance.

"With all that, are you going to have time to drive your Stanley in the parade?" asked Betsy.

"Oh, yes. But I'd like to ask to drive it close to the back, so if something comes up, I'll either have it already handled or can cancel without disturbing the order of the parade."

"Couldn't Jill drive?" asked Betsy, making a note. Lars and his Stanley Steamer were famous in Excelsior; it would seem peculiar not to see it at this event.

"Not with two little ones to watch over," said Lars. "They'll be riding in it, of course, along with the mayor."

Jill and Lars had two children, toddler

Emma Beth and a new infant son, Erik.

The next agenda item was a surprise. Billie called on Ryan McMurphy, who had been sitting quietly in his booth. He rose and came to the table. Ryan was about thirty-five, or maybe younger — years of heavy drinking had lined his face and given him a paunch that his faded blue jeans could only underline. He wore an open red plaid flannel shirt over an old black T-shirt. His hands were thick and a little grimy, but he looked freshly shaven and his dark brown hair was slicked back.

"Well, I guess she's ready to rock 'n' roll," he announced in a sandpaper voice. "The fire truck, I mean," he explained when he saw some puzzled stares. Their faces cleared. Ryan had found an ancient fire engine in a shed on an abandoned farm a few years ago and had been restoring it. He claimed it was the first motorized fire truck in Excelsior. It dated back to the early twenties, and if he was right, it was a piece of Excelsior history. He had offered to drive it in the Halloween parade. His offer had been accepted — if he could get it running reliably.

"Got 'er so she starts right up and runs pretty smooth," he continued. "Kind of noisy, but reg'lar fire trucks don't have mufflers, so that's all right. I found a bell —

31

might even be the original bell, it's got 'Excelsior' cut into it, but no date, or it might be a school bell. I got the ladders cobbled back together, but you can't climb on 'em, they're just for show. An' I can't get the siren to sound right; sounds like it's got a head cold."

He looked around the conjoined tables and a smile slowly formed. "An' guess what? Joey Mitchell came for a look at the truck, and he heard that siren, an' he says it sounds like the ghost of a siren. Then he says the fire department was cleanin' out their storage area and found a dozen old rubber coats, like they used to wear? He says they're half rotted, sleeves fallin' off, and he says he can get 'em for nothin' and if we give 'em a coat of white paint, and get four, five men to wear 'em ridin' on the truck, then . . ." He stopped and looked around the table again. "See?" he demanded, raising his hands. "Don'cha *see?*"

Betsy suddenly saw. "Why, I think that would be terrific! A 1923 fire truck, a creepy siren — and ghost riders!"

Then the rest of the committee saw, too, and there were excited exclamations. Praise was heaped on him, and Ryan stood basking in it for a minute, then said, "That's all, I guess," and went back to his booth. He took a sip of his Coke and looked everywhere but at the committee, still smiling.

Betsy was smiling, too. As she looked around the table, though, she was surprised at the expression on Billie's face. It was of extreme satisfaction. Obviously she was pleased that Ryan had come up with such a great idea for the torchlight parade, but what was she so smug about?

Betsy wondered if the fire truck's ghost riders had been Billie's idea. How nice of her to let Ryan take the credit!

Two

Ryan's fantastic idea made the next item to be discussed, the Men's Precision Folding Lawn Chair Marching Unit, seem mundane by contrast.

But as usual, the discussion surrounding it took longer than anyone wanted, though no one seemed inclined to give up his or her chance to voice an opinion.

They were into a deep discussion of whether the unit would supply its own music from a boom box or just move to whatever the band ahead of them was playing, when the door opened and a man with a withered left arm came in, shaking rain from his shoulder-length hair. He wore a dark leather jacket, jeans, and boots.

"Hello, Joey!" called Billie. "What brings you out?"

"A sandwich and a beer at The Barleywine," the man replied cheerfully. Eyeing the crowded tables, he remarked, "Looks like business is good."

"No, it's a meeting of the Halloween Committee. Give Roger your order." Billie tilted her head toward the bar, where the young man stood, putting silverware away.

But Joey had caught sight of Ryan in his booth. "Hey, Rye!" he called.

"Joey," said Ryan in a wary voice.

Joey swerved toward the booth but didn't go all the way to it. "Whatcha drinkin'?" he called over the sound of a committee member talking.

"Coke."

"Coke?" Joey sounded surprised.

"Coke!" Ryan spoke in a defiant tone.

"Hush, you two!" ordered Billie. "We're trying to have a meeting here."

"All right, all right," Joey said, and quietly to Ryan, "Buy you another?"

"Okay."

"Want something to eat?"

"Nah."

That made Betsy look at her watch and wait impatiently for the committee member currently speaking to stop. When he did, she asked Billie, "How much longer are we going to be here? It's after five o'clock. We were supposed to be done by now."

Billie looked distressed. "Is it five already? We're not even halfway through the

35

agenda." She lifted the sheet in her hand and turned it over to show it to the committee. Some of its members groaned softly, not having noticed that the back side had as long a list as the front.

"All right, settle down, whining isn't going to help any," she said. "But how about we take a break? I'll bring us all a snack and something to drink. Or would you rather just keep working?"

As usual, this set off a discussion, which might have gone on for some while if not for Betsy. She reached back in her memory for remnants of Robert's Rules of Order, and said loudly, "I call the question!"

"What does that mean?" asked someone.

"It means she wants an up or down vote on the question," said Billie. Betsy was surprised; she didn't think Billie would know. "Which is, snack or work?"

"Snack!" shouted half the committee, and most of the others nodded or shrugged acquiescence. The two who disagreed sighed but said nothing.

Roger, whom Betsy recognized as Billie's older son, came from behind the bar with a tray bearing an assortment of crackers and cheeses, and tiny sourdough sandwiches filled with chicken salad. He put it at the junction of the tables and pulled out a note-book.

"First drink's free," announced Billie. That broadened the smiles.

"Summer ale?" requested someone.

"Out till next summer," said Roger.

"Red ale, then."

Betsy was dismayed when almost everyone ordered beer or ale. Nothing, in her opinion, was more likely to further slow things down than a round or two of beer.

She ostentatiously ordered apple cider, and because she was thirsty, she drank almost half of it at once before she realized it was hard.

To soak it up, she ate a miniature chicken salad sandwich and two crackers — the cheese on them was a pale Irish cheddar — and asked for a cup of tea.

A few minutes later Roger came back with her tea and another tray laden with oranges and apples. "Dessert," he announced without a trace of sarcasm.

Billie said, "Did you bring something to Ryan?"

"No, was I supposed to?"

"Well, it doesn't matter. Here, I'll do it." Billie rose and put three of the tiny sand-wiches into a paper napkin. She took them and the orange she had picked for herself over to the booth. Joey had already been served a huge roast beef sandwich and a very large glass of dark ale.

"Thank you," said Ryan, surprised, when presented with the food.

"You be sure to eat that orange," said Billie in a fussy mother voice.

"Yes, ma'am." He smiled — he had a very sweet smile — and made a little show of digging his fingernails into the skin of the fruit.

Billie came back to the table, and the meeting resumed its slow drag.

About half an hour later Betsy's eye was caught by Joey coming back from the bar. He had two of The Barleywine's extra-tall mugs, brimful with beer so dark it was almost black, the heads scanty and cream-colored.

Guinness? wondered Betsy. She had thought The Barleywine served only beers made right on site. She glanced over at the board on which the varieties were listed and realized it wasn't the famous Irish stout but The Barleywine's own Don't Be Afraid of the Dark Ale.

But why had Ryan switched from Coke to ale? It must have been because Joey was buying — small-batch brews were more expensive than commercial brands.

Two hours — two hours! — later, the meeting was finally drawing to a close. Even the most die-hard opinion wielder was now more anxious to go home than to make her opinion known.

"And now, the last thing," started Billie to a chorus of relieved sighs, "is parking for the horse trailers for the Sheriff's Posse —"

She was interrupted by a man's voice singing in a slurring baritone, "For it's *witchcraft, wicked witch*craft, and al*though* I *know* it's strictly *taBOOOOOOO* . . ."

When Betsy saw Ryan McMurphy slide clumsily out of the booth a minute earlier, she thought he was going to leave. Instead he was walking unsteadily toward the bar, voice raised in song. The sweet smiler was gone; this man had a wicked gleam in his eye. Leona had relieved Roger, and was talking with one of the three men in casual office dress sitting on stools, when she heard him and looked up, alarmed.

"It's such an ancient *pitch,* but one you'll never *switch,* for there's no meaner *witch* than you!" Ryan was gesturing theatrically at Leona as he approached, paraphrasing the actual lyrics of the song.

Billie quickly rose and moved to intercept him, but he made a surprisingly deft dodge to avoid her. Ryan went to an empty stool and leaned across it, bracing one hand on the rounded front edge of the bar.

"I'll have a pint of porter, please," he said, careful of his pronunciation.

"Oh, Ryan, for corn's sake!" said Leona. She looked over at his vacated booth, where Joey was sitting with a half-empty glass of stout, looking surprised. "You know we don't sell liquor to you anymore! Has Joey been buying for you? Well, no more. I think it's time for you to go home."

"Oh, yeah? I don't gotta. An' I jus' wanna let you know, Leona Cunningham, I'm still, I'm still on ta you." He pointed a thick forefinger at her.

"Well, I'm glad to know that, but we're still not serving you," said Leona in a calm voice. Like Billie, she wore a dark blue Barleywine T-shirt under her light-colored apron.

He turned fast to grin fiercely at Billie, who, standing too close behind him, took a step backward. But she said bravely, "I also think you should go home, Ryan." Her voice was hard and tight.

"Why? My money's as good as anyone's!" he said.

"Because you're drunk." Billie looked around Ryan at Leona. "I thought we

40

agreed we weren't going to serve him any liquor."

"I haven't sold him a beer all evening," said Leona.

Joey Mitchell called from back in the booth, "My fault!"

Ryan executed, badly, a complicated bow toward Joey. "An' I . . . I thank you."

"Plus," said Leona to Billie, "you're the one who invited him."

"He told me he quit drinking."

"An' you 'nvited me to talk 'bout the fire truck," said Ryan. "So now what, you gonna try an' throw me out, Billie Leslie Lesbian?"

Billie, who was in fact married and a grandmother, said, "You want me to call the cops like we did last time you were drunk in here?"

"You an' what army?"

"Awwww, Ryan, why don't you go home and sleep it off?" growled the largest of the three men occupying bar stools.

Ryan, without warning and with amazing swiftness, struck the man on his shoulder hard enough to knock him off the stool. This made the other two men climb down and back into a corner, where they stood on reluctant alert for a brawl.

Leona suddenly had a very small baseball bat in her hand.

Lars rose from his place at the committee table but just stood behind his chair, watching.

Billie reached into an apron pocket. "That's it, I'm calling the cops right now," she announced, bringing out a cell phone.

"Now wait, now wait, I ain't done nuthin'!" shouted Ryan. "It was a accident! Anyway, it was self-defense! You put that away, jus' gimme a beer and we'll forget, forget all about it." He bent to help the fallen man to his feet. "There, see? No harm done."

"Don't touch me!" said the man, but not loudly, shrugging off Ryan's hands. He backed away to join his companions in the corner.

"Go home, Ryan," counseled Leona.

"I can't. An' you know I can't," he said, his voice suddenly turning sad.

"Why not?"

"The wife threw me out."

Betsy, sitting in riveted silence with the rest of the committee, had forgotten that. She had seen his wife at church two Sundays ago, sorrowful and angry, two shamed-looking little girls with her. It was enough to make a person think prohibition wasn't such a bad thing.

Ryan was saying, "Come on, gimme,

gimme a beer. Jus' one ver' little one?"

"No," Leona said. She had put the bat down but not away. "Where are you staying?"

"In Shelly Donohue's basement. Got a nice room down there."

Betsy was shocked to hear this. Shelly was a local school teacher who also worked part-time in Crewel World. The "nice room" was doubtless Shelly's sewing room. Who had persuaded Shelly to let him stay there? Betsy could not imagine Shelly volunteering to do such a thing.

Leona said, "It's stopped raining. Why don't you walk —"

"No," Ryan said sullenly. "It's cold out, an' I'm thirsty. Gimme a beer — gimme a beer an' I'll go."

"We're not going to do that."

"For Chrissake, it won't hurt you to be kind to a thirsty man! Harv has a kind heart, he'd give me a beer if I asked him. Him an' Shelly, they're *good* friends, like a port inna storm — not like you!"

That's right, thought Betsy. Shelly's boyfriend had moved in with her. His name was Harvey Fogelman.

Ryan's tone had turned belligerent again. "Witch woman!" He glared at Billie. "I bet she's converting you to be a witch, too, ya

43

little witch! A *lesbian* witch, the worst kind! The kind that'd let a man die of thirst, wouldn't even spit on him if he was on fire with thirst." He sniggered. "Thassa good one."

"Listen to me," said Leona and he turned clumsily back to face her. She leaned just a little bit forward, drawing his bleary attention. Her voice was low and intense. "Walk over to Shelly's, Ryan. Walk. It's only three blocks away. You're right, she and Harvey are your friends, and you need a friend right now. You're tired, you could use some sleep. Your eyes are all red, and your face is flushed. You're tired, very tired, you must surely want to walk just those few blocks in the cool evening air, then lie down. You want to lie down and sleep, you need some sleep."

He started to nod in agreement, then his eyes widened in alarm.

"A hex! You're trying to put a hex on me! No, no, no you don't!" He reached into his jeans pocket and pulled out a metal ring, heavily laden with charms ranging from a rabbit's foot to a pewter, Egyptian-style eye. He jingled this so wildly at her that she backed away. "Ha! You know it, you know this blocks hexes!" He repeated the gesture. "See? I bet it burns your eyes! Now, come on, Burning Eyes, try again, try ta hex me!

44

You think I'm Adam Wainwright? No way! Come on, take your best shot! I dare ya! I *double dog* dare ya!" He laughed raucously, then stopped abruptly. "I didn't think so!" he concluded, less certainly, because she was merely looking coolly at him. He turned toward Billie, who had put on the same cool expression. "Hah, hah, hah!" he sneered derisively and made his uncertain way to the door.

"Hold it, McMurphy!" said a voice so laden with authority that Ryan halted instantly. Even in plainclothes, there was no mistaking Lars Larson for anything but a cop.

Ryan said at once, "I'm not drunk," a lie so patent that several people snickered.

"Maybe not," said Lars agreeably, "but your license is suspended. You're not driving tonight."

"Who says I'm driving?"

"I saw your car out front," Lars said. "How did it get here unless you drove it? Give me your keys." He held out one very large hand.

Ryan looked at the hand for a few seconds, then up at the square-jawed face with its implacable sea gray eyes. When exerting his authority, Lars looked very much like a man whose ancestors had gone a-Viking.

Without another word, Ryan reached into his shirt pocket and pulled out a small set of keys.

"These the only ones you have?" asked Lars, taking them.

"What, you think my protection ring can start my car?" retorted Ryan.

"Fine. Come down to the station with a friend who has a license and I'll give these back to you," said Lars.

Still without saying anything, Ryan turned and went out, pulling the door shut hard behind him.

Lars returned to the table and so did Billie. The Committee heaved sighs of relief. Once again, Billie tried to conclude the meeting, but her words were cut short by a squeal of tires braking too hard and the ugly crunch of metal being torn and crushed.

Before anyone else could even decide to move, Lars was out the door. The men who had been sitting at the bar ran out after him, as did Joey Mitchell. The other committee members rose as one.

After about a minute, Betsy went to the door. Cars had stopped in the street, their headlights shining in a pouring rain. A wind had sprung up, turning the rain into silver lances splintering on the street and sidewalk. A dark sedan and one of those pickup trucks so big it had twin tires in back had collided. The car, naturally, had gotten the worst of the encounter. It was facing the wrong way, apparently having been struck with enough force to spin it around. Steam was coming out from under the crookedly lifted hood and fluid was making a puddle under the engine compartment. One front tire was no longer vertical. The truck, which was white and had a farm or company name on its door, was still running, a streamer of exhaust fluttering out. Its bumper and right front fender were crumpled and torn.

Lars, accompanied by one of the men from The Barleywine, was speaking through the broken window to the driver of the car. It was clear from the slow patting gestures he was making that he was telling the driver to sit still — and another patron was on his cell phone, doubtless summoning an ambulance.

But then Lars stepped back, the car rocked slightly, and the passenger door opened.

Ryan McMurphy stepped out, raised his arms in a touchdown stance as the ring of charms — which had proved an excellent cover for a set of keys — tumbled over one hand, and gave a victory cry so loud Betsy

47

could hear him all the way over to the brew-pub door: *"Ta-dah!"*

THREE

"I wish they could keep him — but of course he'll be out as soon as bail is set." Shelly Donohue was speaking as she examined a small overhead projector for sale in Betsy's shop. It was late Friday morning. She was trying to keep her voice calm, using the projector as an excuse not to look at Betsy, but Betsy could sense her anger and frustration.

"I'm just amazed that Ryan wasn't injured in that accident last night," said Betsy. "I suppose it was because he was so drunk." She remembered how often she'd read of drunks climbing out of car wrecks without a scratch on them, a phenomenon no one could explain. Ryan had certainly been celebrating his near escape, though his triumphant stance in the glowing, rain-lanced street had quickly been taken down by the strong grip of Lars. Ryan had only added to his problems by struggling to break free.

Betsy gestured at the projector, which was sitting on top of its box. "This is the last one I have, but it's been here so long I'm prepared to cut you a deal in addition to your employee's discount just to get rid of it." Designers often used a projector to cast a picture onto a piece of even-weave fabric or canvas. Shelly, after years of stitching, was moving into designing cross-stitch patterns.

"It's good news for me, I suppose, that there aren't a lot of pattern designers in the area." Shelly was about thirty-five, more striking than beautiful, with lovely big eyes and masses of brown hair pulled into a careless bun. Her figure was voluptuous and there was a long string of brokenhearted third and fourth graders in her educator past. She was divorced, childless, and she shared her house with a sweet dog, and, currently, with her live-in boyfriend, Harvey, whom Betsy had not met.

Shelly turned from her examination to say, "I actually believe Ryan has a guardian angel who specializes in drunks and fools. Of course, he'll tell you it's the hundred and one protective charms he carries."

Betsy said, "I should have been suspicious when Lars asked for Ryan's keys and Ryan pulled that little ring out of his shirt pocket. But he said there were only charms on the big ring. I wonder how long he's been carrying two sets of car keys?"

"For about a week less than people have been demanding his keys when he's drunk — which is for the last two years, at least. How much for the projector?"

Betsy named a price a fraction over her cost, then said, "I bet you're right about the angel. When he climbed out of that smashed car and did his little dance, I was just amazed. But I had to laugh when Lars reached out and took hold of him. He looked so surprised — I guess his talismans aren't proof against police officers. I heard he was charged with driving under the influence, resisting arrest, driving with a suspended license, and failure to yield. The bail on that should be substantial. Maybe he won't be able to afford it."

"I wish. I know he called Harv to ask him for a loan, but I happened to pick up the other phone when he called, and I told Harv he better not spend one nickel on that man." Shelly sniffed in frustration, not anger. "But Ryan will manage. He always does. He's a senior auto mechanic and they make good money. You know, that surprised me."

"What, that he's held on to a good job?" Betsy was leading the way to the cash register.

"No, that he got drunk last night. After Luella threw him out, he really seemed determined to quit. He'd been sober for almost two weeks — I wonder what happened?"

"Now I think about it, at that meeting he'd been praised for getting that fire truck fixed and coming up with the idea of ghostly firefighters. So it's funny he fell off the wagon, isn't it? And why did you take him in anyway? Because he promised to stay sober?"

"I didn't want to take him in at first. I was too mad at him on Luella's behalf. She's a nice woman and Ryan gets really ugly when he's drunk. But Harv and Ryan went to community college together. Who would've thought the 'old school tie' mentality reached all the way down to a community college?" She laughed just a little, mostly at herself for sounding like such a snob. "But I agreed to it because Ryan swore up and down he'd quit drinking for keeps. I think Luella making him leave home was a real wake-up call for him. He loves her, and loves his kids." She paused as if to gather her thoughts, then shrugged away whatever those thoughts might have been. "What's the total?" she asked, gesturing at the items on the checkout desk.

She'd selected two pieces of canvas, three colors of canvas paint — the kind that doesn't rub off easily or run when it gets wet — three squares of eighteen-count linen, a square of fourteen-count Aida cloth, a tablet of graph paper, and a pair of Gingher scissors.

"Do you need floss?" asked Betsy.

"No." Shelly leaned forward to murmur, "A manufacturer is supplying the floss."

Betsy's eyebrows lifted, then she smiled and guessed, "Hershner's?"

"Kreinik. But you didn't hear me say that."

"Of course not. But will you let me see it before you send it?"

"All right. I'll want your opinion, and maybe Goddy's, too. That should be in about a week; it's almost done. But you must both promise —"

"Of course, not a word. How exciting for you!"

"This is my *third* commission!"

Betsy quoted, " 'Once is happenstance, twice is coincidence, three times is a conspiracy.' "

Shelly laughed. "May it never end!" She

paid for her selections and left. Betsy gazed after her with a happy look, but then her expression grew troubled. Ryan was sleeping in Shelly's sewing room, a room that Shelly hoped to make the center of a new career. How disruptive was that? She wondered how Harv had persuaded Shelly to permit it. The house was Shelly's, after all, not Harvey's. She must be really smitten with him. No matter, Shelly wasn't going to put up with this invasion of her workspace for long — especially now that Ryan had fallen off the wagon.

The Monday Bunch, six strong today — Emily, Bershada, Jill, Alice, Phil, and Doris — gathered at Crewel World on Monday afternoon. They came in shivering, shaking raindrops off their umbrellas and coats, complaining about the weather.

"You'd think we'd get just one good fall weekend!" lamented Emily. "Morgana Jean's play group has been trying to have a fall picnic since the beginning of September! Poor thing, she's so disappointed!" Since Morgana Jean was barely four, it was likely that the disappointment lurked more in the heart of her mother than in her own.

"It's the middle of October, so we probably won't be able to have it outdoors now," she continued. "Hi, Betsy," she added as she settled down in her chair.

"I've got spiced apple cider heating up in back," said Betsy. "The coat rack's back there, too," she added, and Jill led the way to the tiny back room, where the coffee urn waited, along with the tea kettle — currently heating apple cider spiced with cinnamon and cloves — and china and paper cups and mugs.

"Well, Leona did say we were going to have a cold, wet fall," said Bershada, coming back with a cup of steaming cider. She said it lightly and without looking at anyone as she led the way to the big library table in the front area of the shop. She sat down, lips slightly pursed, still not looking at anyone, and got out a wooden frame holding a large rectangular piece of counted cross-stitch. It was a half-completed alphabet sampler featuring bright-colored flowers, from amaryllis to zinnia. A retired librarian, she was doing it as a gift for the Excelsior Public Library.

There was a little pause while Bershada put on the magnifying glasses that rested near the tip of her small nose and the others seated themselves around the table and mulled over whether to take the bait being offered.

Alice, as bold as she was blunt, said, "I do hope we aren't going to talk about Leona and her witchcraft." She was a widow and the oldest member of the group. Well into her seventies, she was nevertheless a vigorous woman, big-boned and broad-shouldered, with a deep voice. She sat down, opened an antique carpet bag, and produced yarn, a crochet hook, and a half-completed afghan square.

"Why not? Our television weatherman said this past weekend would be partly cloudy with a slight chance of rain," said Godwin. "Leona is always better than he is at predicting the weather." It had, in fact, rained steadily all weekend. Betsy raised an eyebrow at him. He had been hoping to hear what the Bunch thought of the Ryan Mc-Murphy incident, but Betsy didn't want hurtful gossip aimed at Leona. He wasn't sitting at the table himself, but was standing at a rack of counted cross-stitch patterns with religious themes, setting in new ones by numbers the shop had assigned.

Betsy was seated at the big old desk that served as a checkout counter, carefully punching credit card numbers into her laptop. The shop's card reader had unaccountably died on Friday, and she had instructed her staff to write down the numbers by hand. A replacement machine wouldn't arrive until Wednesday, so now she had the task of sending the information over the Internet.

She was muttering bad words under her breath because one number wasn't being accepted. It had been written down wrong — and it was a number Betsy had taken down herself. Already two other credit card holders had gone over their limit and Visa was not accepting the charges.

Hearkening to the sounds of angst, Jill twisted around in her chair. "When you get tired of mere words," she said to Betsy, "you can ask Leona Cunningham for something more potent, you know."

There were stifled gasps and giggles around the table. Godwin contributed a patently false gasp and a shake of his blond head in a denial of his own.

"Oh, posh!" said Jill, turning back and fixing them with a cool blue stare. "Isn't that what we're leading up to here? Witchcraft as practiced by Leona Cunningham?"

"No, of course not!" said Emily, but her cheeks were pinking. "None of us believes in that stuff."

"I think some of us do," said Doris in her pleasant sandy voice. She and her beau, Phil, sat side by side, no longer pretending

57

in public to barely know one another. They were each working on a needlepoint Christmas stocking. "It's been all over town that Ryan McMurphy taunted Leona — and Billie — in The Barleywine on Friday, then got hit by a truck three minutes later. I'd say half the people in town think the two things are connected."

"No, they think it's fun to pretend the two are connected," said Bershada. "Like going to a scary movie: you're scared, but not really. Phil, for example, doesn't really think Leona Cunningham put a curse on Ryan McMurphy that came true."

Phil said, "Now, ordinarily I wouldn't believe such a thing, especially of such a nice woman as Leona. But Ryan is such a terrible drunk, and after the way he behaved in The Barleywine, maybe he's not wrong to be worried." He wore a superior sort of smirk as he said this, and Doris nudged him in rebuke.

Emily said, "If Ryan is scared, he's taking a funny way to show it. Did you hear he broke through the screen into Leona's back porch and trashed it? She had flower pots and bundles of dried flowers stored back there, and he kicked and smashed and threw stuff everywhere."

"When did this happen?" asked Betsy,

surprised.

Phil looked at Doris. "Saturday night?" She nodded. "Yes, Saturday night. I'm surprised you didn't hear about it."

"You sound pretty sure Ryan did this, Emily," noted Jill, glancing also at Phil. "How do you come to think that?"

Jill used to be a police officer, and she still had that polite but implacable look a traffic cop can summon at will. Confronted by her cool stare, Emily confessed, "Well, I'm just assuming it was Ryan. But really, who else could it be?"

"What do the police think?" asked Phil.

"They're investigating it as a hate crime," admitted Jill, who would know, of course. Her husband was Police Sergeant Lars Larson.

"Poor Leona!" said Emily.

Bershada said, "I wonder if those were not dried flowers, but dried herbs. Leona has a wonderful herb garden, so this must be like she lost her whole summer."

Emily said, "I bet she was *furious!*" Then she looked guilty.

"Now, Emily —" said Betsy in a warning tone.

But Doris said, "I'd be furious if someone got into my needlework stash and tore things up."

"Yes, but *you* can't throw a hex on the person who did it," said Phil.

"Neither can Leona," said Alice. "Nobody can, there's no such thing as hexes." Her late husband had been an extremely orthodox Lutheran minister.

Betsy stopped entering numbers long enough to say, "I agree. Plus, I think you're all in danger of being cruel and stupid to say such things about Leona, even in fun. She's a very nice woman, and most of you know that."

"Of course we don't really believe in hexes!" said Godwin. "That's why we're joking about it."

"I suppose that's true," said Phil. He took a thoughtful look at his stocking — a present for Doris. It depicted Mr. and Mrs. Claus in the front seat of a Stanley Steamer, a stocking specially designed and painted to his order by local needlepoint artist Denise Williams. Doris, retired herself, had a boiler license and they shared a knowledgeable interest in Lars Larson's Stanley.

Phil leaned sideways to admire her stocking. It depicted Santa driving a steam locomotive — Phil was a retired railroad man. The stocking in her hands was, of course, a present for him.

They had become accepted as a couple in

town, seen everywhere together, without passing through that public-kissy-face stage. Perhaps because they were seniors, it had been an old-fashioned courtship; since they were only engaged, not married, they even maintained separate residences. Doris gave a fond glance at the sapphire and diamond ring on her finger.

Jill said, "Some people believe in curses." She was nearing the end of stitching a counted cross-stitch pattern, of a black cat sitting on a jack-o'-lantern while licking its paw. "That's why what happened to Leona is being investigated as a possible hate crime."

Bershada said, "I heard Ryan invoked Adam Wainwright's name in The Barley-wine when he was raving at Leona about hexes. And you have to admit that what happened to Adam was very strange."

A little silence fell around the table. Adam Wainwright had been a financial counselor in Hopkins, and Leona had invested fifty thousand dollars of her husband's life insurance with him. A couple years later, needing the money to set up the microbrewery, she discovered that all but a few thousand dollars of it had disappeared. Adam told an investigator that Leona had instructed him to invest in high-risk stocks and the money was lost when the investments went sour. Leona denied Adam's story, but the man produced documents with Leona's signature on them and so he was never charged with a crime. Soon after, he was driving his classic Corvette convertible around Lake Minnetonka when an eagle flying overhead dropped a huge bass, which landed squarely on Adam's face, causing him to swerve off the road. The car was totaled, and fish scales got into his eyes and caused an infection that essentially destroyed his vision. It was a shocking, weird accident, and some of Leona's friends felt it couldn't have happened to a more deserving person.

"Do you mean to tell me that any of you sitting at this table thinks Mr. Wainwright's accident was caused by a curse put on him by Leona Cunningham?" demanded Alice in an awful voice.

"Ryan believes it," said Godwin. He pushed another pattern into the row of them on the shelf, and turned to face them. "And right after Ryan accused her of it, he goes out and gets his car wrecked. This despite all his amulets."

"What are amulets?" asked Emily.

"Haven't you seen that collection of his?" Godwin used his hands to form a softball-size shape in the air. "It's got so many good-luck pieces on a big silver ring that if he ever fell into the lake, it would take him right to the bottom."

"Oh, that Ryan is just silly!" pooh-poohed Emily, her knitting needles flashing. She was making a sweater for her toddler son. "She made him mad, telling him to walk home. Of course he felt he just had to drive his car, and so he blames her for the wreck."

Bershada laughed, but Jill said, "That sounds just like excuses I've heard from drunks back when I was on patrol. 'She told me I couldn't, so I had to prove I could.' And he probably doesn't remember doing the vandalism to Leona's back porch. He's been drunk ever since he got out of jail."

"He knew what he was doing when he dared Leona to put a hex on him at The Barleywine," said Betsy, remembering.

Godwin said, "Even if he thought his lucky charms protected him in that accident, it seems stupid of him to tempt her again by trashing her back porch."

"Of course, his accident had nothing to do with the fact that he was severely intoxicated that evening," said Alice repressively.

"It had everything to do with it," said Jill. "Being drunk also gave him the nerve to beard the lioness in her den — stand up to Leona in The Barleywine."

Phil said, "I heard he jangled that key-chain right in her face and dared her to lay a curse on him."

"Did she?" asked Emily. "Lay a curse? You know, did she say the words that meant she was cursing him?"

"No, of course not," said Jill. "She told him to walk, not drive, *walk* home and sleep it off."

"Were you actually there?" asked Doris, hearing a note of authority in Jill's voice.

"No," said Jill, "but that's what's in the police report. I also happen to know Ryan blew a two-oh."

"What's that mean?" asked Emily.

"When they make you blow into a little machine that measures how drunk you are," said Betsy, "it comes up in numbers."

Jill said, "In Minnesota, oh-eight — that is, a zero-point-zero-eight percent blood alcohol level — is legally too drunk to drive. Zero point two zero is very drunk."

Betsy said, "He must have had a lot more beer than we realized. I wonder why Joey Mitchell kept buying it for him."

Bershada asked, "Aren't those two good friends?"

"They used to be," said Phil. "Then Joey was in a car accident with Ryan behind the wheel. Joey came away with a smashed left

64

arm that'll never be right. He had to quit the fire department because of that, and I know he was mad at Ryan for a long time."

"He must have gotten over it, then," said Betsy, remembering how Joey greeted Ryan warmly and came to sit with him in The Barleywine booth.

"How'd Ryan get drunk?" asked Bershada. "I heard Leona and Billie agreed never to sell him any more beer after that night he got in a fight and broke their jukebox."

"Joey bought it for him. He admitted it."

"What was Ryan doing there in the first place?" asked Emily.

"He'd come to tell the committee about having finished restoring that antique fire engine for the parade," said Betsy.

"What would one point zero be?" asked Doris, idly curious.

"Dead," Jill said. "I read not long ago of a woman who was zero point five seven and she is considered a medical miracle because she came out of her coma and lived."

"Why would anyone drink till they nearly die?" asked Emily.

"Usually on a dare or a bet," said Jill.

"Chug-a-lug, chug-a-lug," chanted Phil, nodding at an old memory.

Betsy frowned at him. Where had she

heard that recently? Not directed at her, but overheard. Probably from someone at The Barleywine.

The subject was wandering away from superstitions, so Godwin said, "Look, a Hamsa Hand." When they all looked toward him, he held out a counted cross-stitch pattern with a color photograph of the completed piece on its front. It looked like an open hand, blue, palm forward, with three fingers between two thumbs, all pointing down. In the center of the palm was an eye with a red heart for an iris. Above the hand was printed a line in some very foreign language. "Ryan has one of these in pewter," he said; "I've seen it myself."

"What does the writing mean?" asked Doris.

Godwin consulted a tag hanging on a string from the bottom of the canvas. "It's Hebrew for 'Let this home be filled with the blessing of joy and peace.' " He seemed disappointed that it didn't say something like, "May this home be safe from hexes."

Betsy said, "The Hamsa Hand is also found in Arabic countries. There, it's the Hand of Fatima."

"Muslims and Jews have the *same superstition?*" asked Emily incredulously.

"Actually, the hand is older than either

66

religion. But sometimes Muslims and Jews will wear the hand as a sign that they want reconciliation."

"Why is there an eye in the palm?" asked Doris.

"It's protection against the Evil Eye," said Godwin, looking again at the tag.

"It *looks* like an evil eye," noted Alice.

"But it has a heart in the center of it," objected Emily.

"There's many an evil deed done in the name of love," remarked Jill.

"Do you believe in the Evil Eye, Goddy?" asked Betsy in a very dry voice.

"No, of course not," said Godwin, making cabalistic gestures with his free hand and pretending to spit left and right. Phil and the women at the table laughed, even Alice. Godwin often made grand, brave statements he would simultaneously contradict with a gesture. It was part of his insouciant charm.

"Are you superstitious, Betsy?" asked Phil in a jocular voice.

"Oh, no more than average," said Betsy, trying for a distracted voice, picking up the next sales slip. She didn't have any amulets on her keychain, but there was a small, real amber bead sewn into the lining of her swimsuit. Sailors knew that wearing an amber bead means the wearer will never die by drowning. In another life, Betsy had been a Navy WAVE.

Godwin decided to become direct. "Do any of you really believe Leona Cunningham is a witch?"

"Of course she is!" said Emily, staring at him. "Isn't that what we're talking about? She's a Wiccan."

"No, I mean, do any of you believe she can cast a spell on someone?"

"Well . . ." said Phil, scratching the underside of his jaw with two fingers. "There's more things under heaven than most of us realize. We Christians believe in miracles, so maybe we should believe in the opposite, too . . ." He shrugged.

"Oh, stop it, Phil!" said Alice. "I can't believe you think there's anything in such silly superstitions. To think that in this day and age *anyone* would believe a person can boil up a potion of bats' wings and tiger talons and harm another person with it is too ridiculous even to contemplate!"

"Bats' wings and tiger talons?" echoed Emily. She began to giggle. "I thought it was eye of newt and toe of frog."

"Well, whatever it is. No mortal human can harm another with fairy-tale rhymes and a . . . a kind of nasty soup."

Emily's giggle became a laugh.

Alice continued doggedly, "It's wicked to spread belief in such nonsense. I should think responsible people would speak up against it."

Doris said, "I think that when people are harmed by curses, it's because they believe in them. I've read that if a person truly believes in witches and warlocks and such, and a witch throws a curse on him, he will actually get sick or even die just from believing in it."

"Do you think Ryan got in that accident last week because he truly believed Leona put a hex on him?" asked Godwin.

"I agree with Jill — Ryan got into that accident because he was drunk," said Doris.

"And mad," amended Phil. "Leona told him he should walk home, so of course he had to show her she wasn't the boss of him. Except he didn't."

"How could he go home?" asked Bershada. "I thought his wife threw him out."

"I forgot about that, Bershada!" said Emily. "You're right, she did. So where was he going? Does he have a place to stay?"

"He's living with Shelly," said Betsy. "Apparently her boyfriend is an old friend of Ryan's and he talked her into it. It would have been an easy walk, even in the rain." She remembered the hypnotic tone of

Leona's voice as she told him to walk the three blocks to Shelly Donohue's house.

"I wish Shelly could join the Monday Bunch," said Doris. "I love it when she's working in here, and I've been admiring her designs. It would be very interesting to watch her work out a pattern."

That set off a discussion of favorite designers. Emily loved Barbara Baatz-Hillman — her pillows ornamented her daughter Morgana Jean's bed. Phil had recently added Stoney Creek's patterns, "Railroad Memories," to his stash.

Jill was singing the praises of Jane Greenoff when the door sounded its two notes and Leona Cunningham came in, her dark eyes enormous in her white face. She was without a coat or an umbrella and was streaming wet, a condition she did not seem to notice.

"Betsy," she said in a trembling voice, "I want to talk to you."

Betsy stood. "Of course." She led Leona into the tiny room at the very back of the shop.

"Ryan McMurphy has been found dead."

"Oh, my God. What happened?"

"I don't know. But someone just called me to accuse me of murdering him."

"What? Who?" demanded Betsy angrily.

70

"I couldn't tell. But don't people know? I would never, *ever* use the craft to harm anyone!"

"Of course not! We know that!"

"Someone doesn't."

"Oh, someone's just being stupid and cruel. But how did they know?"

"It was the third caller to tell me the news. It's probably all over town. Betsy, can you help me find out who it was? This sort of thing can take root and spread."

"Yes, it can. All right, I'll do all I can."

"Thank you."

FOUR

Betsy walked Leona to the door, and as soon as she had left the shop, Betsy turned to the waiting group of stitchers. "Ryan Mc-Murphy is dead. Someone called Leona to tell her."

"Dead?" echoed Emily, looking frightened. "But we were just talking about him."

"And Leona," said Godwin.

For a few moments there was silence, then Jill pulled out her cell phone and punched a speed dial number. "Where are you?" she demanded when it was answered, and her face went still while she listened. "When?" she asked, then, "What do they think?" Jill had a champion poker face, but her brusque tone and too-stiff expression caused the others to watch her impatiently until she hung up.

"What did Lars say?" asked Alice, successfully guessing, along with everyone else, whom Jill had called.

"He says Ryan McMurphy is dead, all right."

"Strewth!" exclaimed Godwin, and groans of dismay swept the table as the news was confirmed.

"What's worse, he was found in Shelly's sewing room."

"Sweet Jesus!" exclaimed Phil.

"God have mercy on us all," said Alice, bowing her head.

"Amen," said Godwin, shaken. He had known Shelly longer than he'd known Betsy.

Betsy asked, "What happened? Was it . . . murder?"

"No, thank God," said Jill. "He didn't turn up at work this morning and didn't answer his page, so his boss called Shelly's cell to see if she knew what the problem was. She didn't but volunteered to go home on her lunch break to see if he was there. At the house, she went down to check his room and found the door locked and no answer when she knocked. So she used her key to open it. She found him on his futon on the floor. He wasn't breathing and she couldn't rouse him, so she called 911. From the state of the body, they think he died sometime last night."

"What did he die of, then?" asked Emily.

"They're thinking heart attack, or possibly

73

acute alcohol poisoning. There's no mark of violence on him."

"Ohhhhh," sighed Betsy, relieved. "That's — well, it's not okay, but at least it's not suspicious." She looked at Jill. "Right?"

"They'll do an autopsy, but I'm guessing the alcohol did it." Jill looked at Phil. "Chug-a-lug."

Phil looked abashed. "I wasn't wishing that on him, you know!" He looked around. "I wasn't!"

Betsy said, "We know that. But it's awful. If he was that sick from drinking, I wish he'd signed himself into a treatment center."

Jill said, "It's interesting that he wasn't taken to Detox when he got arrested last Thursday." Detox was a clinic under county contract to care for people in the grip of severe intoxication. Drunks were brought there to sober up under medical supervision.

"Well, he was walking and talking at The Barleywine just before it happened," said Betsy. "And he gave Lars a pretty good fight when he tried to arrest him. So maybe they thought he was just drunk and disorderly, not in danger."

"Besides," said Godwin, "that was Thursday. He died three days later, last night."

"Don't you have to be drunk for weeks to

74

die of it?" Emily asked. "He was sober for a week or more before he went on this binge, right?"

"Well," said Jill, "normally a person will drink for years before his body breaks down under the load. On the other hand, a person drinking for the first time can drink enough in one evening to injure or even kill himself. I don't think Ryan was in serious trouble. I do know the Department's been kind of keeping an eye on him, cutting him off at the pass when they see him drunk in public, but that's because he's a nuisance drunk."

Bershada snorted. "Nuisance? That's putting it politely!"

"Yes, but when he's sober, he's fine," said Jill.

"Was," said Godwin. "He *was* a nuisance, he *was* fine. Now he's dead."

The silence that fell this time was less thunderstruck and more reflective.

"I wonder who called Leona to tell her she was a murderer?" mused Betsy.

"Is *that* why she was so upset?" demanded Godwin.

"Yes."

"How incredibly gauche and rude!" said Bershada. The others agreed, but the news set off a round of gossip as everyone slowly got back to the normality of stitching. There was no consensus on who might have done it. Ryan was well known in Excelsior for his wildly aggressive drunk personality, only a little less well known for his friendly and helpful sober one. Drunk or sober, he was volubly, often ridiculously, superstitious, and the Monday Bunch agreed he seriously believed Leona eager — and able — to put a curse on him.

"So then whoever called Leona agreed with Ryan probably," said Doris. "Who do we know who would believe that?"

"Hold on," said Jill. "Some people just like to stir up trouble."

"I think it was that friend of his, Joey Mitchell," said Emily. "He's probably pretty upset about Ryan's dying, and he knew Ryan had a problem with Leona. Plus, those two have been friends since high school."

"Not so much since that accident a few years ago," said Bershada. "It was Ryan driving the car that smashed Joey's arm."

"They were both drunk that night," noted Alice.

Betsy said, "Joey seemed friendly enough to him in The Barleywine the other night. Sat with him and kept buying him beers."

"And I suppose Ryan bought a round or two himself," said Godwin.

"No," said Betsy. "But that was because

he wasn't supposed to be in The Barleywine in the first place. Billie and Leona banned him after he got drunk and belligerent a time or two. He was only there because he was invited to tell the committee about the fire truck being ready for the parade."

Godwin, who fancied himself a bit of a sleuth, said, "How about this: Ryan ruined Joey's arm, so he got Ryan drunk on purpose, hoping he'd get into an accident and ruin *his* arm and not be able to work anymore?" No one seemed to think much of his idea, so he went back to the original question and said, "I think Irene Potter called Leona to tell her she was a murderer. That is just the kind of thing she'd do."

There was a soft, guilty laugh of agreement around the table.

Irene was Excelsior's most famous resident artist. With Betsy's encouragement, she had started selling her very eccentric needlework, first at art fairs, then at local galleries, now to art museums. Her work was brilliant but unsettling. Betsy recalled in particular a flower garden with an evil-looking snake winding its way among resplendent blossoms. Her mind was as eccentric as her work, and she looked at human activity from an angle few others could achieve. Godwin was among the first to see how phenomenal her work was, but that didn't stop him from laughing at her theories about why people acted as they did. That Irene was as avid a gossip as any person in town only added to his amusement.

"Well, now we know there's not a chance in hell Leona had anything to do with Ryan's dying," said Phil. "Irene hasn't been right about anyone, ever."

The others were not sure about that, on the stopped clock theory, but still they chimed in with their opinions on who made the call to Leona. Since actual information was lacking, this was a fruitless exercise. At last, Phil picked the least likely person he could think of: Alice. "She's been lying to us, y'see," he insisted, smiling impishly at her. "She's more superstitious than all the rest of us put together, but she pretends she isn't. Just ask to look in her purse; I'll bet you'll find a membership card in the Old Wives' Tale of the Month Club."

Everyone laughed more comfortably, and on that note the meeting began to break up.

For a wonder, it wasn't raining, nor was the wind blowing a gale. Daylight was fading, but the sky was clear and that deep blue only autumn can turn it. Godwin and Rafael stood at one end of the driving range. They both looked good in gray wool pants and brightly patterned sweaters, and there was something pleasant about the darkness of one and the fairness of the other. Rafael had golf shoes on, but Godwin wasn't sure he really wanted to become a golfer, so he wore sports shoes in a shade of silver-gray that matched his trousers. They were using Rafael's clubs — the two men were less than two inches apart in height, so the clubs fit both of them. The driving range was for irons only and had green canvas signs marking distances of fifty, a hundred, a hundred and fifty, and two hundred yards. It was level, with four slightly raised greens complete with flags.

"You're not really supposed to use a tee on the fairway," said Rafael, "but I find it helpful sometimes. And it was very helpful when I was a beginner." He pushed a white tee into the sod and placed one of the range's orange balls on top of it. "Now, remember what I said about your swing. The ball should not be centered between your feet, but toward the forward foot. Put the club just behind the ball. Keeping the left arm straight, lift the club back, past the level of your right shoulder. Then . . ." Bringing the club down in a swift but not effortful movement, Rafael connected with the ball. With a sharp *click,* it flew down the range to land on a green a hundred yards away. "See how I follow through," he instructed, and Godwin tore his admiring eyes away from the distant green to see his friend standing in the classic golfer's twist, right foot up on its toes, club over his left shoulder. "Always follow through," he repeated, and handed the club, a five iron, to Godwin.

Godwin was athletic, partly because he liked being active and partly because it helped him keep an illusion of youth — he was perilously close to thirty but didn't look over twenty-three. He played tennis, bocce, and a killer game of croquet, could swim and dive, owned a bicycle (though he rode it only on cool, sunny days), and did just enough of any of this to keep himself slightly buff. So why couldn't he get the hang of this golf business? Just hit the ball with the stick. Not the ground behind it, not the air above it, not just the very tip-top of the ball so that it fell off the tee and rolled an embarrassing few feet away. He bit his lower lip, balanced his ball in place — after three tries and a resetting of the tee — and silently reciting Rafael's instructions, took a mighty swing. To his amazement and satisfaction, the ball went flying. Okay, off to the left, but more than fifty yards down the range.

"Well done!" cried Rafael. "I believe you are going to be better than I!"

Godwin started to laugh; he couldn't help it. He looked into Rafael's bright brown eyes, kind and amused, and both of them began laughing. When they finally stopped, and after Rafael sent a ball flying nearly two hundred yards, Godwin decided to try hitting the ball without a tee and, to his immense satisfaction, sent it nearly seventy yards. Maybe he would get the hang of this stupid sport after all. He hoped so; it was Rafael's passion.

Later, in the clubhouse, over hamburgers and beers, Rafael said, "There is something about your boss you have alluded to that rouses my curiosity. Among her other talents, it seems she is also a detective. Is this really true?"

Godwin, unable to speak because of a mouthful of meat and bread, could only nod.

"And is it also true that she will investigate the mysterious death of Ryan McMurphy?"

Godwin shook his head, swallowed, and said, "No, the death is mysterious, but the person who will find the cause is the medical examiner. This isn't a murder; it's a medical mystery. Betsy isn't a doctor."

"She could investigate the *bruja*." Seeing Godwin's incomprehension, he translated for him. "Sorceress."

"What are you talking about?"

"What is the word? Oh, *witch.* You have a witch living in Excelsior, am I not right?"

"You mean Leona? She's not a witch, she's Wiccan."

"Now I do not understand. What is Wiccan?"

"Wicca. It's a religion. I think it's called an 'earth religion,' because its practitioners believe in things like spirits and goddesses. But she doesn't go around in long black dresses, or ride on a broom, or cook poisons in a cauldron by the light of the moon."

"But does she cast spells?"

Godwin grimaced. "Well . . . I think so. She believes in magic, I'm sure. But only to make good things happen. She says it's terribly wrong and dangerous to try to hurt someone with a spell, that it can backfire on you three times over. She makes herbal things, potions and soap, and nice-smelling dried bouquets. But she's not a wicked person, she's nice. No one could believe she's a wicked witch. I mean, she's a *stitcher!*"

Rafael laughed softly. "You are amazingly

sweet and somewhat naïve, you know that? She is not wicked, but she calls it Wicca." He leaned closer and said, "Do you know my favorite quote? It is from Shakespeare, from his play *Macbeth,* and it goes, 'And oftentimes, to win us to our harm, the spirits of darkness tell us truths, win us with honest trifles — to betray us in deepest consequence.' "

Godwin smiled and said, "If you could taste Leona's beer, you wouldn't think it an 'honest trifle.' "

Rafael said, "You are a . . . cheeky person, do you know that? May I give you a nickname?"

Godwin was instantly interested. "All right, what is it?"

"*Gorrión.* It means 'sparrow.' "

Godwin couldn't keep from looking a little disappointed. "Sparrow?"

"When I was a young man, a sparrow flew near me and I reached out my hand without thinking and caught him. He was a cock sparrow, very small in my hand, and I held him up to my face for a closer look. I could feel him struggling to be freed, but instead of being frightened, he reached around and bit me on the thumb. '*¡Bravo, Gorrión!*' I said, and released him."

"You think I'm brave?" Godwin sat up a

little straighter.

"I know it, *mi pequeño Gorrión*."

FIVE

Sergeant Mike Malloy took brief notes as Dr. Rendelle reported his findings. The doctor, Hennepin County's assistant medical examiner, was short, and so obese his stiff movements seemed more a result of tight-fitting skin than a natural reflection of his character. He didn't make eye contact once during the conversation. "After a superficial examination, I could find no cause for Ryan McMurphy's death," he said, his speech as stiff as his movements. "He was very intoxicated, point one eight, but that is not a lethal level. An autopsy may disclose more."

"So speculate for me, what do you think happened?" asked Mike, taking notes.

"I think an autopsy will tell us more," repeated the doctor, not caring to venture an opinion, looking somewhere over Mike's left shoulder.

Mike turned to make sure there was no one else in the chilly white room.

The doctor continued, "I'll know more after I have a look inside him, run some more tests. You did say he was a heavy drinker, right?"

"Yeah, and for Ryan, a BA of point one eight is serious but he's still up and talking at that level."

"Prolonged alcohol abuse can damage a person's organs — heart, liver, stomach — so that a relatively mild binge could put him over the tipping point. Though at that stage, there are generally more signs of it externally."

"Ah," said Mike, nodding and writing. "Time of death?"

"Well, I'd estimate time of death at between two-thirty and three-thirty a.m. Monday morning." Mike looked expectant and so the doctor, searching for something more to contribute, said, "There is what appears to be a cigarette burn on the sole of his left foot."

"What do you make of that?"

The ME looked slightly exasperated. "That the man, who was barefoot when found, stepped on a lit cigarette."

"That's funny, because it was too cold outside to go barefoot, and there wasn't a cigarette burn on the floor of Ms. Donohue's sewing room." It probably wasn't important, but Mike wrote it down, because it was odd and you never knew. "Well, thank you, Doctor. Let me know when you're ready to do the autopsy."

"I'll do that."

Malloy, a medium-tall fellow with dark red hair and freckles thickly strewn across his thin-lipped face, sighed as he went out to his car to begin the tedious work of finding out about Ryan's last hours.

Shelly, called out of the classroom, was interviewed with her live-in boyfriend, Harvey Fogelman, who'd been called away from his job at Exterior Artists, an architectural firm.

They said they were in bed asleep when Ryan came in, and so had no idea what time that might have been.

"So he has his own key?" asked Mike, notebook at the ready.

"Well, he has a key to the room he sleeps — slept in," said Harvey, whose craggy features were the deep bronze color only hours in the outdoors can bring. Mike had discovered that Harvey was a landscape architect. Whatever "landscape architect" was, Harvey's role was a great deal away from the drawing table.

Shelly continued, "We almost never lock

our doors, unless we're going out of town for a weekend or longer, which didn't happen while he was living with us. But I made a copy of the key to my sewing room so he could have some privacy when he was in there."

"He was supposed to stay with us just for a few days, at most a week," Harvey put in, with a glance at Shelly. By the look Shelly was giving him, Ryan's being allowed in the house at all was a deal made between Harvey and Ryan over Shelly's objections.

"And instead, how long did Mr. McMurphy stay?" Mike asked.

"It would have been three weeks tomorrow," she said tightly. "I wouldn't have been so angry about it, except that he fell off the wagon. He got drunk every night starting last Thursday. I don't know what started him drinking again. I believed him when he said he would quit. And then . . . this." Her voice rose higher than usual, with more vibrato in it. She clearly was very upset — understandably so, since she was the one who came home to find the body. *And* in her sewing room.

Mike remembered a favorite aunt who had a room set aside for her quilting and knitting. It was a holy place; he was allowed in there only rarely. And once in, he had to step carefully, not touch or spill anything. So he could see how much worse it would be to have someone using the sacred place as a bedroom, much less to lie down and die in it!

"I believed him, too," said Harvey in his deep, calm voice. "I would never have invited him to camp with us if I thought he'd overstay his welcome or get sloppy drunk every night."

"Do you know where he'd go drinking?" asked Mike. "I'm trying to find out who saw him last."

"No," said Shelly, shaking her head. "His car isn't parked around here, remember? Your men went searching for it but couldn't find it. So maybe it was a friend who gave him a ride home from wherever he was last."

"But we don't know who the friend was," said Harvey.

"Maybe it was Joey," Shelly suggested to Harvey.

"Joey?" asked Mike.

"A drinking buddy. I don't know his last name. He used to be a fireman until his arm got messed up."

"Ah, Joey Mitchell. Thank you." He wrote that down, thanked them, and left.

Joey Mitchell worked for an insurance adjuster, and when Mike arrived at his office, he said he was overdue for a coffee break. He took Mike to a small break room empty of other employees, and they sat down on flimsy plastic chairs at a Formica table.

Joey hadn't brought Ryan home Sunday night, nor could he think offhand who might've done so. But he did know McMurphy's watering spots. He named Haskell's in Excelsior, and then some bars east of town. His favorites used to be — and probably still were — in Minnetonka and Saint Louis Park, two Minneapolis suburbs about fifteen and twenty minutes from Excelsior, respectively.

He was shocked at Ryan's death but not really saddened. "We used to be good friends," Joey said, "but not so much since I cut back on my boozing." Mike wrote that down, too, and headed out.

He found Ryan's car in St. Louis Park. It was in the little lot behind Ralph's Happy Hour. The bartender on duty hadn't worked last Sunday. He called the night shift bartender, who remembered the seriously drunk Mr. McMurphy being accosted by "this guy who comes in about four times a week." The bartender thought his name might be Waylon. The day bartender said, "Oh, he means Waylon Halverson."

Halverson's wife said he was at his day job as a mechanic at an import motors shop on Thirty-Sixth Street. Mike found him bent over a Peugeot's open hood and summoned him outside, where they stood under cloudy but not rainy skies.

"A crazy drunk named Ryan? Yah, I see him now and then. Off-and-on kind of guy, sobers up for a couple weeks, then he goes on a bender, then he sobers up. Me, I drink just a little, but steady. I'm in Ralph's Happy Hour about every other night."

"Did you see Ryan in Ralph's Happy Hour on Sunday night?"

Waylon nodded. "Yah, as a matter o' fact. I been out with the guys and was the last one still there when he came in, really pis— uh, drunk. He gets to this weird stage when he's drunk, where he thinks there's some kind of plot against him by someone with secret powers."

Mike screwed on his most doubtful face. "A plot? By who?"

"Oh, nothin' human. He says there's these spirits and hexes and all kinds of crap floating around out there, and he's some kind of magnet for 'em. He carries this steel ring with about a pound of rabbit's feet and four-leaf clovers and even weirder junk on it, says it's his 'protection.' " Waylon snorted

91

derisively.

"Did you talk to him?"

"About that? There's no talking to him about it, all you get is a rant."

"Well, about something else then? On the Sunday, I mean. What did he say?"

"Just that he was fine, he was going to be fine. But he wasn't, he was about as drunk as I've ever seen him. And real, real nervous."

"About what?"

Waylon shrugged. "The usual. Witches and black magic. More nervous than usual, but it was the same old story."

Mike nodded comprehension, and asked, "Was he barefoot when you saw him, or did he take his shoes off while you were with him?"

Waylon stared at him in surprise. "No, why?"

"It's not important. Do you know where he went when he left the bar?"

"He went home. I know that because I took him."

Mike nearly smiled in delight. Here was a truly solid piece of information.

"When was this?"

"About eleven-thirty we left the bar, so I'd say he was back in Excelsior around midnight, maybe a little before."

"Why did you take him home?"

Waylon snorted. "Because he was drunk on his a— butt. He tried to fool me with that second set of car keys, but I was on to that trick. Fool me once, *shame* on ya; fool me twice, shame on *me*." He rested his bottom on the fender of an arrest-me-red Porsche and shoved both hands into the pockets of his pale blue coveralls. "So I took both sets and made him ask me nice for a ride home. He laughed half the way because I caught him over that trick, and cried the other half."

"Why did he cry?"

"Because he wasn't living at home but at a friend's house. His wife threw him out because he's so obnoxious when he drinks. He said he tried to quit drinking but someone set him up to get back on the sauce."

Mike asked alertly, "Who?"

"He didn't say. Or maybe he did, I wasn't really listening. He's likely to say anything when he's drunk. I took him to this little house in Excelsior, he got out and I gave him back his keys, and I watched him stumble up the steps and go inside."

"Do you remember the address?"

"No." But when he described the house and its general location, Mike recognized it as the Donohue residence.

93

About then it occurred to Waylon to ask, "What's this all about anyway?"

"Ryan McMurphy was found dead in that house around noon on Monday."

Waylon straightened and pulled his hands out of his pockets. "He was? What happened?"

"We're not sure yet."

"I bet he fell."

Again that alert feeling. "What makes you say that?"

"A friend of mine took a guy home who he thought was drunk, and the guy died in his bed, and it turned out he had fallen earlier in the day, smacked himself good on the head. He died in his sleep from bleeding inside his brain. He'd fallen down. He wasn't drunk at all."

Mike opened his notebook. "To your knowledge, did Ryan suffer a fall?"

"No."

"Did he tell you he'd fallen?"

"No. But listen, I wasn't with him all evening. He came into the Happy Hour already drunk. Or else having a stroke."

"Did he smell like alcohol?"

"Hell, yes! But that could be why he fell, because he was drinking."

Mike wrote that down because it could be true, thanked the man, and left.

■ ■ ■ ■

Betsy had been assembling little holiday cross-stitch kits — each with a poinsettia pattern, fabric, floss, six gold beads, a needle — to sell at her checkout desk when Billie Leslie came in. Billie was an avid stitcher and, like most, always working out of season. Betsy was glad to be able to tell her that a kit she had ordered had come in. Bee's Magic, it was called, and by the photograph on the outside of the packet, it was a surreal marvel. Worked on black, it depicted a broken-down picket fence entangled in morning glories and raspberry canes with a strange mix of birds, bees, butterflies, mice, and even a hedgehog sitting on a mushroom — a fantasy of a hot summer at nightfall.

"Would you consider letting me display this when it's finished?" Betsy asked. Well-done models created orders, and Billie was a very competent stitcher.

"Well, let's see how it comes out first," said Billie. "It's kind of at the far end of my skill, working on black. Listen," she went on in a different tone, "I want to ask you what you'd think if the parade —"

She was interrupted by a *bing-bong!* as the

95

doorbell chimed and in came a short woman with nervous mannerisms and black hair that stood up in little curls all over her head. She paused inside the door to look around, her shiny dark eyes alert.

"You've changed things around," she said in a sharp, accusing tone.

"Hello, Irene," said Billie in a cool voice. To Betsy, she added, "I'd better get going, I've got errands to run."

"Thank you, Billie," said Betsy, waving good-bye as the woman left. "Hello, Irene!" she continued. "You haven't been here in a while."

"Haven't needed to," said Irene briefly, still looking around.

Betsy came out from behind the big desk that was her checkout counter. Her smile of greeting began to feel a little false. "What can I do for you?"

"It's what I can do for you," replied Irene, pleased to have thought that retort up all by herself. She opened a flat, black canvas bag and brought out a piece of folded linen dyed in uneven shades of purple. She brought it to the table and unfolded it. The darkest shades were at the top, fading quickly to uneven swirls of pinky lavender across the middle. It was an angry sky dotted with little clusters of X's, like leaves blown in a stiff wind. Near the top, just under the darkest purple dye and cradled in a thin, uneven line of purple cloud, was stitched a white sliver of moon.

"I dyed it myself, and I can get you all the yardage of it you want," she said.

The bottom quarter of the fabric was also stitched — mostly cross-stitches — in browns, tans, and grays scattered with vertical stitches that made Betsy think of a weedy lawn or garden in late autumn. In the center was a big leafless tree — the knobby, crooked limbs proclaimed it an oak — and stuck rakishly on an upright limb was . . . Betsy bent closer over the design.

A witch's hat. From a lower branch, lifted into a curve as if in a stiff breeze, hung the skeleton of a fish, and among the lifted roots of the tree was a half-buried but very realistic human skull.

The design looked simple at first, though a second look showed an alarming number of color changes in the trunk and limbs of the tree — and in the grass and weeds, too. It was a striking design, but an eerie one. Betsy had a number of Halloween designs in her shop. Next to Christmas, it was the most popular seasonal design theme. But only rarely were the Halloween patterns seriously spooky, and none as disturbing as this.

"I call it 'The Witch's Tree,' " said Irene.

"It's very striking —" Betsy began.

"I've already turned it into a pattern," Irene went on, talking over her and reaching into her bag and producing three sheets of stapled paper. "I think it should sell really well, particularly in this area, don't you?"

Betsy felt a stir of anger. "What do you mean, 'particularly in this area,' Irene?"

"I mean, after what's been going on in Excelsior, the falling fish and mysterious death and our very own witch living right in the midst of us."

Betsy had to take two deep breaths before she could control her impulse to shout, so it was in a deadly calm voice that she asked, "Irene, did you call Leona Cunningham and accuse her of murder?"

"Oh, no, of course not! I would never do such a thing! How can you think I would do such a thing? I would never accuse her of anything! What if I was wrong? What if she recognized my voice? She might . . . cast a . . . do something . . ." Betsy was relieved to see Irene at last pick up the signals Betsy was sending. Her words stumbled and ran down into silence.

"Do you believe in witchcraft, Betsy?" she

asked in a falsely cheerful voice.

"No, I do not. Do you?"

"Well, not really. I mean, there's good witchcraft, right? Blessings and herbals and, and, and — *beer!* That sort of thing is real. But not curses and hexes and other black magic, that can't be real. It's just make-believe. That's why we like Halloween nowadays, right? It's just make-believe wickedness, like ghosties and ghoulies and long-leggedy beasties and things that go bump in the night, good Lord deliver us." Irene gave a brief, high-pitched giggle. "Does this mean you aren't going to sell my design in your sweet little shop?"

"Irene, this is a wonderful, powerful design," Betsy said, hedging a bit. Not that it wasn't true. "How did you find that perfect fabric?"

"I found it at Stitchers' Heaven, that shop in Dinkytown that went out of business. Fifteen yards of white congress cloth at fifty cents a yard, would you believe it? Then I bought some pink dye, orange dye, and dark purple dye and played with the colors. I found that if you do small, concentrated batches, then thin it without stirring, you can take a paintbrush and kind of swoop it over the fabric and create these great effects. Like this sky. I did the pink first with just a tinge of orange, then the purple at the top. I was going to try for a sunset — do a little more gold with the pink and orange coming up from the bottom — but I liked this so much I stopped here. It looks like an *angry* sky, don't you think? And all swirly, as if the wind is blowing a gale."

Betsy nodded. "Yes, a very interesting effect."

"And at first I just thought about a late-fall storm, but then all this business with Leona and Ryan happened, and I looked at my pattern and it simply *inspired* me!"

"To do the tree?"

"Oh, I was always going to do a tree, they are so interesting, don't you think? Especially without their leaves. No, to do something . . . witchy."

"So you do consider this piece a charge against Leona for trying to cast a spell on Ryan McMurphy." Betsy tried to keep her voice calm.

Irene, oblivious, nodded. "Yes, of course. And on Adam Wainwright, too. But in a *fun* way, don't you see?"

"Don't you think that's a cruel thing to do?"

"Well, it's a joke, and jokes are almost always cruel, isn't that so? And considering what she did — or *thinks* she did to

Ryan . . ." Irene made a kind of nudging gesture while blinking rapidly. "I'm glad you understand what I'm trying to do with this design. I can only hope others do, too."

Betsy sighed. If only that were not so! Shop-owner Betsy wanted to buy the pattern, which was so striking she was sure it would sell well; but citizen-with-a-conscience Betsy would do no such thing. Beyond the obviousness of the design, Irene, who was as dotty as a spotted dress, would very likely explain the motive for her design to anyone who would stand still long enough to hear it.

Betsy searched for a tactful way to turn down Irene's offer. She did not want to start an argument that might end with Irene losing her temper. Even in a calm state, Irene was a little scary, and Betsy did not want to be alone in the shop with Irene in a rage.

"I'm sorry, Irene, but I couldn't give this the prominence it deserves at present. I'm about to take down all my Halloween things and set out the Christmas designs and patterns. On the other hand, I would be honored to debut it in Crewel World — next year. I could feature it in an ad, do a story about it on my web site and in our newsletter. Maybe do an interview with you, if you would be so kind. This could be a bestseller, you know; you have the most remarkable talent for evoking emotion as well as reality in your designs."

Irene simpered and blushed at the praise, though it was amply deserved. It would be wonderful to have a design by a famous needlework artist offered to the public for the first time — Irene had never turned any of her work into a pattern before. To have it debut at Crewel World would be a real coup. It could be, as the saying went, a win-win-win. A win for Irene, for Betsy, and for all the stitchers who patronized the shop.

But then Irene began to look crestfallen. "I wanted it out this year," she said. "It would be more timely that way."

"I understand that. And I'm sorry, but it's too late to do it properly this year. I mean, think about it, Irene. If I bought a dozen patterns from you and sold even as many as eight or ten, that wouldn't make it worth your while. Besides there is work still to be done. You need to turn these pages into a booklet, and get it properly printed. And you'll want a color photograph of the model for the front, right? Plus you need to get the fabric cut to size — and if you're going to include the fabric, you might want to kit it up properly and include the floss. This will take a lot of time and cost you a certain amount of money. You don't want to do all that for such a small return. I think this should go to a needlework publisher, one with the resources to give it the attention it deserves. I can't believe there aren't a whole lot of other needlework shop owners around the country who would be very happy to offer it. I hope you will remember me when it is published, because I would love to debut it in my shop. Let's think about doing that next year. You should aim for a date in, say, mid-August."

"I'll think about it," said Irene, a bit petulantly, folding up her model.

The door went *bing-bong,* and Betsy looked around to see Godwin coming in from a late lunch.

"Hey, Irene!" he said chirpily as he entered. "What brings you to our precinct?"

"Precinct?" she echoed, a little alarmed, as if Godwin were threatening her with the police. So maybe she did have an idea that there might be more than one kind of danger in accusing a Wiccan of murder.

He gestured around the shop. "To our district, our area, our little world?"

Betsy said, "She's designed a cross-stitch pattern, a gorgeous thing. She wants us to sell it in the shop."

"*Really?* A pattern? Can I see it?" He

hustled to the table and took the folded cloth from her hand.

Betsy knew Irene didn't like Godwin, partly because of his slanted sense of humor but mostly because he was gay, and she was afraid of gay people. On the other hand, he was a very gifted stitcher with an excellent sense of design, and she had come to appreciate that. So after a brief tussle, she opened her fist and let him take and unfold her work. He smoothed it with both hands onto the table and there was a breathless silence.

"Oh. My. God." He cocked his head first to one side and then to the other. He stepped back and came close and bent very close over it and stepped back again. "Irene, this is *genius!* It's *marvelously* spooky! I *love* the fish! Have you really made a *pattern?*" Betsy handed him the stapled pages. "Why, this is *terrific!* This is actually *doable!*"

He looked at Betsy. "We're going to sell it, of course," he said.

"Goddy, she made this pattern as a kind of commentary on the witch who lives among us."

Godwin frowned at her, then looked again at the pattern. "Oh, my God," he said again, but with a totally different intonation.

Betsy said, "I told her we would like to

104

sell it, but that we're about to put out our Christmas things and so couldn't give it the attention it deserves."

Irene was looking at Godwin as Betsy spoke, so she felt safe raising and lowering her eyebrows and twiddling her fingers over her head.

"Oh, my gosh, I forgot! You're right, all our Halloween stuff is about to go into storage until next year." He looked at Irene. "How about next year?" He looked at Betsy.

Betsy nodded approvingly. "Next year."

SIX

On autopsy, the medical examiner could find no anatomic cause of death for Ryan McMurphy. No clot in the brain, no hidden stab wound, no internal rupture. Essentially, Ryan simply stopped breathing; and after a while, his heart stopped, too. So Dr. Rendelle took a few samples from the body, wrote "Natural" on the death certificate under "Cause of Death," signed it, and released the body.

Ryan was given a quiet, private funeral and tucked away beside his grandparents in Excelsior's hilltop cemetery. His bereaved wife took her two sad children home, where she closed her door against the curious questions of the town and waited for the surprisingly substantial life insurance policy to be cashed in.

But the failure to find a cause of death only increased the talk. Business at The Barleywine dropped off alarmingly, and after a day or two of it, Leona came into Crewel World.

"Betsy, have you made any progress in finding the source of the gossip about me?"

"No, and it's getting worse, isn't it?" said Betsy.

"Yes. There seem to be more people every day who think I am responsible for Ryan's death."

"The medical examiner said in very clear language that he died of natural causes."

"Betsy, he was thirty-four years old, he wasn't weak or sickly, and he worked at a physically demanding job. It's hard not to think there was something unnatural about his dying."

"All right, I'm sure things can be missed even on autopsy. It's possible the medical examiner didn't see a very small tumor deep in his brain, or maybe there was some kind of heart problem that doesn't show. Or maybe it was cumulative. His heavy drinking had to have affected his whole system."

"Then why is this gossip persisting? I'm sure someone is stirring it up. But who? Who keeps saying these ugly things about me?" There was agony in the questions; Leona's dark eyes were filled with anxiety.

Irene Potter, thought Betsy, though she said, "I don't know."

"You've proven yourself a good detective, Betsy. Please, won't you try to find out who it is — and make her stop?"

"Her? What makes you think it's a woman?"

Leona's eyes flickered. "I don't know that it's a woman. It just makes sense to me that it would be."

Harvey Fogelman was concerned about Shelly. Faced with a deadline to finish that design for Kreinik, she nevertheless had abandoned her workroom and instead brought things up to the living room. This put him in the awkward position of trying not to see what it was — it was supposed to be a secret. He knew it was a cross-stitch pattern, but nothing else. But he couldn't help getting glimpses of it when she had it sitting out on the coffee table. She had damaged the edge of the table trying to set up her Dazor light on it, and finally had to ask for his help.

Keeping the project upstairs was a huge nuisance, because she had to keep putting it away when company was coming over. She kept a light blanket handy for when a casual visitor dropped by, and it seemed there were a lot of visitors lately.

There was something Harvey needed to

talk to her about, something urgent and long overdue, but how could he when she was already in such distress? At last he said, "Look, this is driving you crazy. I don't understand why you can't go back to using your sewing room."

Shelly said the room made her uncomfortable and she couldn't work in it while feeling uncomfortable. Harvey couldn't see what the problem was. He had taken the futon to Goodwill and called in ServiceMaster to clean the room from top to bottom. He had rearranged the furniture and even painted the walls a pale blue-green — her favorite color.

This needed to be resolved, and soon.

Now, this morning, he suggested as gently as he could that they both should go down there one more time and she could perhaps explain exactly what was wrong.

So before she had to leave for her teaching job at Excelsior Elementary, they went downstairs. Normally, just stepping inside brought her a feeling of cozy pleasure; he'd seen it on her face before. But he watched her step into the room and stop short, her face expressing trepidation and distaste. Even her long-eared dog, Portia (because she was made of portions of many breeds), stood outside the door, making small whining noises.

"Can't you tell?" she said, turning to him, her eyes filling with tears. "Can't you smell it? It smells of death in here!"

"Oh, sweetheart, there, there, darling," he said, coming in to take her elegant figure into his arms. He could feel her trembling even while at the same time he marveled at how well she fit against him. This affair had to be right; he was really falling in love, he had to do something soon, or there would be a huge explosion, and she would be hurt — he couldn't have that. "There, there," he murmured, stroking her back, inhaling the fragrance of her hair. But how was he going to tell her?

Then he paused, frowned, lifted his head to draw a testing breath through his nose.

"Well, I'll be damned," he said. "You know, you're right. It smells like a dead mouse in here."

As closing time approached, Godwin became antsy, moving around the shop, picking up objects and putting them down, dusting, needlessly rearranging displays. When he was worried or upset, Godwin cleaned. Betsy finally called him on it.

"Is something wrong?"

"No, no, what could be wrong?"

"You seem to be expecting a problem. Do you want to call off dinner?" Now and again one of them would invite the other to a cozy little supper. Godwin had done it this time.

Godwin smiled. "Not a problem."

Betsy smiled back. "Rafael?"

Godwin nodded wordlessly. "You've met him but you haven't really *met* him. I've invited him to dinner tonight, too, so you two can talk."

"All right," said Betsy, "I've been hoping for a chance to have a real conversation with him. It hasn't been all that long for you two, but it seems to be serious."

Godwin tried an indifferent shrug and failed. "It is," he muttered, drawing his shoulders up again.

"Then what's wrong?"

"I don't know."

"Why do you like him?" asked Betsy, both kind and curious and therefore persistent.

"I don't *know!*" repeated Godwin. "And that's the problem. I mean, he *has* met my usual requirements: he's good-looking, he has his own condo, his own car, his own money, and he's not a rich attorney with control problems."

Godwin had lived for a half dozen years with a wealthy attorney who was very controlling. The attorney had had to die for

Godwin to escape the relationship. There had followed a series of young men who seemed more anxious to have regular meals and a place to sleep than to be sincere friends. Godwin had stopped allowing that, but Betsy still felt he set the bar too low.

"Is there a 'but' in there somewhere?" she asked now.

"Yeee-ess, I think so. We get along so well. We're not alike at all, but he makes me laugh, and I can make him laugh, too. We *never* fight — but maybe that's because I'm afraid of getting into a fight. He's *so* wonderful, I'd be just *devastated* if we stopped getting along." Godwin was blinking rapidly in an attempt to hold back tears. "Do you know what he calls me?"

"What?"

"*Gorrión.* He says it means 'sparrow.' Is that good or bad?"

"What does he say?"

"He says it's because I'm small but brave — I think he means 'cocky.' He says he caught a sparrow once, and while it was helpless in his grip, it reached around with its little beak and bit his thumb. 'Brave,' he says. Or maybe he means 'defiant'?"

"I think he means 'brave.'" Betsy touched him on the arm while she thought for a few moments. "Maybe if you're so afraid of breaking up, you should just go ahead and say or do whatever you like. If you do quarrel, it was never meant to be, and if you don't, then you can relax and enjoy his friendship."

Godwin thought about that and then nodded. "Yes, I see what you mean. A relationship based on false premises isn't real and won't last, no matter how hard I try."

"Right."

"On the other hand," said Godwin, like a child dragging at the hand of someone taking him to a place he doesn't want to go, "I really, really like him. I'm ready to do a little pretending if that means he'll stay around. What I would like for you to do is take a good, close look at him tonight. Tell me what you think."

"All right. Goddy, you must know that if you like him, I'll like him."

"Yes. Yes, that's true." But in a few minutes Betsy realized that Godwin was still upset. She saw him in the far back of the shop, scrubbing out the coffeemaker.

Dinner was a success. Godwin could cook only a few dishes, but he did them exceedingly well. He served roast chicken stuffed with herbed bread crumbs and water chestnuts, autumn squash in a butter sauce flavored with sage and nutmeg, and fresh green beans steamed with slivered almonds. Dessert was vanilla ice cream under a hot applesauce he'd made himself with ginger, cloves, and lots of cinnamon.

Godwin's apartment was small and inexpensive, located on the third floor of the old hardware store, now remodeled and restored. He could have afforded better, especially if he'd chosen to live outside Excelsior, but he loved living in this little town — and besides, he was always saving for a trip to Mexico or Costa Rica or Japan or, presently, Italy.

His great sense of style had turned the small place into a little gem of rich colors and shining surfaces.

"I have a great-aunt in Venice," said Rafael, when talk turned toward travel.

"You do?" said Godwin, surprised.

"So you're part Italian?" asked Betsy.

"Yes," nodded Rafael. "That part of the family goes back a very long way, but she and I . . ." He paused. "*Es la última de la dinastía.* That means 'She is the last of the dynasty.' Her name is Sophia." He smiled. "Like your cat. She is not unlike your Sophie, at that. She is large, gray and white, very manipulative — are not all cats manipulators? — and lazy in such a grand way

114

she makes it seem like a gift." His smile turned a little sour. "She does not approve of me. Oh, not because I am gay, there are always gay people in any family. But because I refuse to marry. She says of course I might have a boyfriend instead of a mistress. To preserve the dynasty, she thinks I should marry and have a son. But I will not do that to a good woman."

"Good for you!" said Betsy.

"Still, it's kind of sad," said Godwin, and the look Rafael gave him made Betsy's heart turn over in her breast. Godwin had said he was afraid he had nothing in common with Rafael. Betsy could see that was not true. Godwin had an understanding and compassionate nature that was shared and appreciated by his new friend.

Leona wrapped things up in the microbrewery — checking the specific gravity of the pumpkin beer brewing in the fermentation vessel, then washing all surfaces and rinsing thoroughly. The secret to beer, the real secret, she knew, is cleanliness. A stray bacterium or a single wild yeast getting into the brew could spoil it entirely.

Then she went around the pub, checking doors and lights and alarms. Satisfied all was in order, she pulled on her raincoat —

of course it was raining again; it was going to mostly rain until it mostly snowed.

Walking the several blocks home, she considered her earlier conversation with Betsy. She liked the woman, and trusted her, but this afternoon had not been the time to mention that it was the Tarot that told Leona her enemy was female. Betsy was a good Christian and so probably not much of a believer in such things. If Leona wanted Betsy's sympathetic help in this wicked gossip business, she had better not make a display of her psychic powers.

She went in her front door and waited to be greeted by her two cats. Snap, a ginger-and-white neutered tom with deep orange eyes, came at a trot and braced himself with a forepaw on her knee to be stroked. "Well, hello, Snapper," she said. "Where's your partner in crime?"

Snap didn't know, he didn't care, could he have another caress?

But Jo-Jo the Dog-Faced Cat was nowhere to be seen. "Jo-Jo?" called Leona. After a few moments, two eyes came glowing to life in the darkest corner of the dining room, under the buffet.

"Say, what's got you spooked, baby?" asked Leona.

In reply, the cat came stiffly out from

116

under the old piece, crossed the dimly shining hardwood of the dining room floor, and walked sedately to Leona. There she sat, just out of reach, looking steadily up at her mistress.

Where Snap was jolly and friendly, a licker of chins and a lover of play, Jo-Jo had the poise and dignity of one of the great cats. She was a solid black, and her shape was that of the long, lean, heavy-muzzled leopard. Her method of communication, unlike the ebullient Snap's, was subtle. But perhaps because she had to work harder at it, Leona could read her better than the tom. By the look in Jo-Jo's eyes, something troubling had happened while Leona was gone.

Leona made a swift pass through the rooms, finding nothing amiss. There was no alarming aura in the house, no strange smells, no disturbance in the air, nothing broken or out of place. The back porch door had been repaired, and was intact. The upstairs, bedrooms and bathroom, was untouched. No window open, no one hidden in the closets.

Leona sat down on the old horsehair couch in her living room and traded stares with Jo-Jo. "Well, what is it? By the Goddess, I wish you could talk!"

Since she couldn't, Leona sat back and let

her psychic talent loose. She had been thinking like a non-Wiccan about the vandalizing of her back porch, a necessary stratagem when dealing with police and other citizens, a "we're just like anyone else" persona she could assume at will — because it was mostly true. But right now it was time to put her witch's hat on and consider things from a Wiccan point of view.

Someone had vandalized her porch and the police were treating it as a hate crime — an attack on her because she was Wiccan. No arrests had been made, and now her cat was all slantwise. She hadn't been slantwise after the first attack, she'd been upstairs under the clawfoot bathtub, where she had remained for twenty-four hours.

So this wasn't as serious. Still, Jo-Jo was alarmed because something alarming had happened. While not as scary as the vandalism, maybe it was a setup for something more serious. And it had happened because Leona had been thinking and acting so non-Wiccan at the time of the first attack. She had let that attitude — and sheer busyness at the pub — prevent her from performing a cleansing ritual in her house and rebuilding the psychic protective barriers around her property.

That was an omission to be taken care of

at once. As in *now*.

She went into her kitchen and opened a lower cupboard fitted with shallow shelves holding canned goods. A hidden latch turned the shelves into a second door, behind which she stored herbal preparations in dried, powdered, and liquid form. She selected three mixtures and poured them into a silver bowl that had a raised pattern of quartered circles, stirring them with her fingers. There were a great many herbs and dried flowers in this mixture, everything from African violet to willow bark. It had an amazing scent, the hops, cloves, and anise the most potent, but dill, onion, and caraway seed doing their part as well.

"I call upon the Goddess in all her aspects," she murmured, "protectress of home and hearth, of crop and livestock, of birth and death, of the welfare of women, the avenger of wrongs done to the earth. I summon Bast and Sekhmet, Freya and Hecate, and all those who would help me make the walls, floors, and ceiling of my house impervious to harm."

She scooped up a part of the mixture and put it in a porcelain bowl, then poured in about half a cup of salt, again blending it with her fingers, and repeating the charm. She went from room to room turning on every light, scattering the mixture on windowsills, door jambs, and into corners. Snap trotted along behind her, eager to sniff at every strew. Jo-Jo came to sit in the exact center of each room as she went into it, watching, but saying nothing.

Finished, Leona went back to the kitchen and picked up a censer — a pierced lidded pot on a chain. With a little effort, she got half a charcoal briquette glowing in the bottom of it. She added crushed white sage and cedar shavings, and the powerful aroma — almost like marijuana — wafted to the ceiling.

"I call upon the Father-God in all his aspects, Tyr, Odin, Thoth, Ganesh, and Thor the Mighty," she said, "and all those who right wrongs, protect the innocent, and repel boarders." Trying not to cough, she censed the house, driving out any evil influences remaining. Then she went back through and opened windows, turning on fans, clearing the air.

Satisfied, she went to the old brick fireplace in the living room, over which hung a battered antique saber used in battle by her great-great-grandfather in the Spanish-American War. She pulled it from its scabbard and whirled it three times over her head, a summoning gesture, invoking both

120

Kali and Shiva, bloodthirsty Goddess and God. She could feel a warmth flow off the sword, down her arm, and into her breast. She went back to the kitchen, scooped up the silver bowl, and went out the back door. She stood awhile in the semidarkness — the lit-up house cast enough light to see by around the weedy yard. It had stopped raining.

Beginning in the southwest corner at the rear of the house, she sprinkled some of the mixture, calling on God and Goddess to stand guard, to cast out malice and evil intent. She erected a psychic barrier (she imagined it as a very tall, thick, gray, stone wall with cut glass and razor wire on top) against those who would harm her, or anything of hers, within these precincts. A believer in angels, especially the kind who had swords, she recited a prayer to Saint Michael the Archangel, the lead warrior of all angels. "Defend us in battle against the wiles and wickedness of our enemies," she prayed. "Cast out those who go about the world seeking the destruction of the innocent. *Selah*," she pronounced at the end of the prayer. Be it so.

She raised the saber, and suddenly envisioned it as flaming. She brought it down hard so its tip struck into the wet ground at the very corner of her property, and began to walk the border, pulling the blade behind her, its tip still stuck in the earth. At the northwest corner she stopped again, sprinkled more herbs, repeated her prayer, then cut a line to the northeast corner, repeated the prayers, then to the southeast, then back to the southwest corner, to complete the circle. She raised the sword again and felt it trembling in her hands as she set the wards, made the protection spell permanent.

"It is done," she murmured then and had to sit down among the soaked thistles for a minute or two as her knees threatened to give way.

With her vision of the real world still blurred and her perceptions altered, Leona did not see the movement of a short, slim figure behind the trees at the back of her lot, slipping away into the night.

SEVEN

"But I did look, and there's not a dead mouse in there anywhere." At the breakfast table, Shelly and Harvey talked about yesterday's discovery of an unpleasant smell in Shelly's sewing room.

"Let me see." Harv hunted and Shelly made another search, without success. Harv went and fetched a claw hammer, and he pried off a section of baseboard near the door, where the smell seemed strongest. To his amazement, not one but two dead mice tumbled out.

"Whuff!" he said, trying not to inhale. Shelly retired to the kitchen. She may have been a strong, independent woman, but she still considered some things to be man's work.

Remembering an old trick, Harvey went up to the bathroom and found what he remembered was in the medicine cabinet: an old jar of Vicks VapoRub. He put a dab under his nose, which killed his sense of smell for anything but menthol, and went back down to the basement.

He pulled Shelly's little desk away from the wall, stooped, and pried another length of baseboard off. There was another mouse in a nest of insulation with her babies, dead. In total, he found four adult mice and four babies, all in about the same degree of decrepitude — and he had a feeling there were more higher up in the wall.

Since Shelly insisted they not use any mousetrap but the old-fashioned kind, with metal springs — much as she hated mice, she couldn't bear knowing of the long suffering surrounding their deaths by poison or sticky-board methods — there should not be dead mice in the walls. So why were they there? And why only in Shelly's sewing room? Harvey did a careful search of the basement, including an experimental pulling away of a section of drywall near the washer and dryer. Nothing, nada, no more dead mice. Nothing upstairs, either.

He told Shelly what he'd found, put the problem in her capable hands, and went off to work, sure she could handle it.

Shelly called an exterminator and explained the dilemma. The exterminator, despite a busy schedule, made an appointment to come out that afternoon, as soon as Shelly got home from work at three-thirty. While as puzzled as she was, he seemed more alarmed.

"You haven't been putting down poison?" he asked on arriving.

"No, we only use traps."

"And this is the only place in the house where there are dead mice?"

"We haven't found any in the rest of the house, and don't smell them anywhere else, either."

But people miss things. He took a careful look himself but found nothing. Still, a lot of dead mice could mean some kind of disease, and sick mice could mean, eventually, sick people.

"Well, isn't this a strange thing," he said at last. "Have you heard from your neighbors about them finding dead mice in their houses?"

"No. But I haven't told anyone about this yet, either. Isn't it strange that there should have been baby mice dead, too?"

"Not if it's some disease. Did you find any dead rodents in the garage or maybe in the grass the last time you were out raking your lawn?"

Shelly's fact twisted up in distaste. "Ish! No."

"Well, maybe it's a coincidence that you found them all in one place. But if some kind of disease did this, it could be the start of an epidemic."

While writing up a report, the exterminator asked her if anything odd had happened in her house about five days ago. "Flood, or gas leak, perhaps?" he hinted.

"A man died in that room last Sunday night. But the medical examiner said it was from natural causes."

The exterminator strongly recommended she report the presence of the dead mice to the Minnesota Department of Health, and gave her their dead bodies in a plastic bag. "They'll want to take a look," he said.

But the first person Shelly called was police detective Mike Malloy.

Jill Cross Larson came into Crewel World that afternoon, a reflective look on her face. Her infant son, Erik, whom she carried in a sling, was making motor noises inside his cocoon of blankets. All that could be seen of him was the rich carrot color of his hair. He was a big baby, seventeen pounds and twenty-five inches long at four months old, and very cheerful.

"Where's Emma Beth?" asked Betsy. Emma Beth was Erik's big sister.

"Preschool," said Jill briefly.

"Already? It doesn't seem all that long ago she was a babe in arms like little Erik there."

"I know, I know. Betsy, I have something important to tell you."

Mildly alarmed — Jill almost never rushed or pressed — Betsy said, "Jill, what is it?"

"They found a pack of dead mice inside the walls of Shelly's sewing room."

Betsy frowned. "I don't understand."

"Whatever it was that killed Ryan Mc-Murphy also killed every mouse hiding in that room, too. *And* a slew of Japanese beetles and box elder bugs looking for winter quarters as well."

"All over the basement, right?"

"No, just in that sewing room."

"Oh, *Jill.*"

"You bet. Someone from the Department of Health went over the house and yard, but the dead critters were all in that sewing room. The medical examiner will be retesting some specimens he kept after Ryan's autopsy, to see if he missed something, and the MDH is autopsying the mice — and the insects." Her smile at this mild jest was frosty.

"So what do you think happened?" Betsy asked.

"You're the sleuth, I never made detec-

127

tive. What do *you* think?"

Betsy thought. "First, I don't think we're talking about natural causes anymore, of course. But what is it, then? Poison gas? No, how would you get poison gas into a room and not get it all over the rest of the house? Some other form of poison, maybe? Suppose Ryan brought some food into the sewing room that was poisoned, and the bugs and mice ate the leftovers."

"I'll ask Lars if there was a dirty plate in the room."

Jill left and half an hour later Police Sergeant Mike Malloy called Betsy. "Are you getting involved in this?" he demanded angrily.

"I think I might have to, the way people keep bringing it up to me," she snapped back, feeling harassed.

"It's just that when you do, things get screwy."

"I know. I'm sure all of us wish this was just what it seemed at first: a man drinks too much and dies in his sleep. But Mike, what do you think about the dead mice and bugs? Isn't that strange?"

"Of course it's strange. But strange things happen all the time." His anger flared again. "Especially when your name comes up!"

"So leave my name out of it," she said in

her most reasonable tone. "But before you do, tell me: Was there a dirty plate in Shelly's sewing room?"

"No. She wouldn't allow food in that room. And I already asked her if he could've fixed something in the kitchen, and she said no, unless he washed the plate and put it away, and he never washed a plate before while he was there."

"And that won't do anyway. He would have needed to bring the poison into the room so the mice could come sneaking out after he went to sleep and eat it. And then the bugs would have had to eat the last crumbs."

Mike said, "The man who brought him home says he didn't have a carryout box with him."

There was a thoughtful silence.

Mike said, "So, what do you think?" Once upon a time, he would have cut out his tongue before admitting he wanted the opinion of an interfering amateur. But Betsy had proven herself competent and useful a couple of times; maybe she could do so again.

"Well, if it's not poisoned food or drink, then it seems to me it could only be poison gas — but how to confine it to just the basement room? Is it airtight?"

129

"Close. The window is tight, and if you stuff a blanket or rug under the door, it might work. But I'm amazed Fogelman or Donohue didn't smell something, or wake up sick the next day. And they didn't. Maybe it's simply someone with a big, soft pillow and a grudge."

"And what kind of teensy pillow would you use to smother a box elder bug?" asked Betsy.

Mike laughed. "Damned if I know. Let me know if you come up with something."

As it often did when word got around that Betsy was working on a case — and in Excelsior, the grapevine was a vigorous plant — the shop was crowded all the next day. People came in to look at the trunk show of Peter Ashe needlepoint canvases, to buy a skein of DMC or Kreinik or Weeks Dye Works floss, to choose among the just-arrived mohair-blend skeins of knitting yarns — or so they would have Betsy and Godwin believe. What they really wanted was to know what Betsy was going to do about Ryan's murder.

They'd all decided it must be murder, even as they decided Betsy must solve it.

"I think it's Leona," said one of the first customers. "Oh, maybe not with witchcraft, but it's Leona, definitely. I don't like her — I never did like her. And now she's a murderer. I guess we should have known."

"We don't even know it's murder, much less that Leona is responsible," Betsy said to her, and to others, over and over. "There may be a perfectly innocent explanation for his death."

Coming out of the back room after making a fresh urn of coffee, Betsy overheard, "There's no such thing as witchcraft!" and brightened.

But, "Yes, there is," came the prompt reply. "I saw it on a television show — it was on The Learning Channel, so it must be true — about psychics and witchcraft and ghosts and everything. They said the police use psychics all the time."

"They do? Well, maybe there's something to it — maybe to some of it, then."

Over by the knitting yarns: "What do they call it? Sky clad. That means they go naked. Even in winter!"

And among the overdyed silks: "Have you ever seen her eyes? There's a strange look in them. She looked at Irene Potter in the grocery story yesterday, and Irene says she went all trembly." But surely no one took Irene Potter seriously.

Billie Leslie came in, and for a wonder

131

just grimaced dismissively at the gossip about Leona. She had something more important to talk about, and it was rolled in a towel in her hand. "Maybe you can help me with this." She unrolled the towel to reveal a piece of dark gray even-weave fabric about twelve by twelve inches. Centered on it, at about ten by ten inches, was a square border made of two rows of cross-stitching in a checkerboard pattern of darker and lighter shades of yellow-green. Inside the border was a complex pattern of white geometric lines, like vines conceived by an Art Deco artist. There was an opening in the center, wider at the bottom than the top.

"Say, that's attractive!" said Betsy. "Where did you get the pattern?"

"I made it up. That is, I think I made it up. I woke up two days ago with it in my head. I may have seen it somewhere, but if so, I can't remember where. You know how that is."

"Yes," said Betsy, who indeed knew how it was. She had often worked out problems with a knitting or cross-stitch pattern in her sleep, waking without memory of a dream but the solution clear in her mind.

"So what's the problem?"

"I've got two problems with it." Billie

132

turned it over to show that the backside of the piece was as flawless a design as the front. "Blackwork is supposed to be the same on both sides. But see, I missed a few stitches."

"Is this blackwork?"

"Yes, of course." Billie seemed surprised that Betsy didn't know that. "Didn't Lisa tell you? It doesn't have to be black on white, it can be white on black, or red on white, or green on purple, even blue on blue."

"I'm afraid my first blackwork lesson is this evening," said Betsy.

"Oh? Oh, I thought you'd already taken the class. Darn. Well, I can't figure it out. I'm not sure it can be done without missing at least one stitch right in that place." Billie touched a spot on the fabric with a disappointed expression.

"Well, can't you fudge it somehow? You know the motto of this shop, don't you? Better done than perfect."

Billie nodded sadly. "Yes, I know."

"Maybe after my class I can be of more help."

"Maybe."

Attempting to cheer her up, Betsy asked, "What are you going to put in the middle?"

"I don't know. That's the other problem."

Betsy felt more confident in helping with this one. "Another border? A square won't fit, will it? And even a rectangle will have the vines coming across it here, I think, unless it's really narrow — but then there will be too much space down here, at the bottom."

"Maybe a triangle?" said Billie, interested now, frowning and looking at the pattern. "No, that won't do, there's still too much room at the bottom. Oh, maybe I should just give it up!"

"No, don't do that, you've done too much work to quit now. And it really is pretty. Here, I've got an idea." She took a scrap of paper and a Sharpie pen and drew three elongated diamonds, shaped into a triangle. "You and your Mitsubishi — don't you see? Look, their emblem fits as if you had it in mind." She picked up Billie's fabric and held it up to the front window then slipped the sketch behind it. A trifle too large for the space, otherwise it fit comfortably into the shape Billie had worked with her vine pattern.

Billie turned her head this way and that, looking at it. "Well, aren't you clever? That's just *perfect.* I'll stitch it in silver and hang it on the rearview mirror!" Billie was very fond of her Mitsubishi.

"And because it's blackwork, it will look nice from both inside and outside the car," said Betsy.

"Yes, and thank you. I only wish I could do it properly, so it's a real piece of blackwork. I don't know why I'm so disappointed in this, it's the first pattern I've ever designed myself. But I wanted it to be perfect."

"Nothing in this life is perfect, Billie," sighed Betsy. She nodded subtly at a customer nearby who was saying, "I never did like Leona, never. There's something *wrong* about her and that so-called 'religion' of hers."

Now that Billie's needlework conundrum was fixed, she could pay attention. She said, "Betsy, do you think it's possible that Leona did put a curse on Ryan?"

"No, of course not!"

"Well, good!" She rewrapped the pattern in its towel and left.

Peggy Dokka brought sixteen skeins of DMC floss to the checkout desk. "Betsy, you have to do something!"

Betsy tried to keep her tone light and ignorant. "About what?"

"All this foofaraw about Leona Cunningham. What everyone is saying — you have to *do* something!"

Alice stepped forward. "Tell them this:

135

There was once a man who claimed he could summon demons using a spell he found in a book, but his friend said about him, 'Yes, he summons them all right. But do they come when he calls?' "

"What does that mean?" asked Kathy.

"It means you can throw all the curses you like, but do they work?"

Another customer snorted indignantly. "Well, I should say this one did!"

A young woman standing behind her ventured, "I had a great-uncle who never had a day's luck in his whole adult life. Everyone talked about it, but no one knew why — except his wife. She said he was cursed and she knew the reason why, but never told."

The first woman said, "There ought to be a law. Seriously, there *ought* to be a *law!*"

Hours later, closing for the night, Godwin said to Betsy, "You didn't mean that, about an innocent explanation for Ryan's death, did you?"

"There may be one, hidden in all the foolishness about a curse. But I don't think so. I think this is a case of murder. What I wish is that every false explanation could be proven wrong, because then we'd know whatever was left is the real explanation. The problem is, even if we knew *how* it happened, would that tell us *who?* Why would anyone want to kill Ryan McMurphy? There were people unhappy with him, I know. But who was murderously angry? Nobody I know."

She wasn't sure what Godwin said under his breath in reply, but it sounded suspiciously like, "Leona Cunningham."

Betsy disagreed. But there were people she would put on that list. Joey Mitchell, for example. A person who found his life's dream spoiled by another man might be angry indeed.

The closing routine finished, Betsy followed Sophie, her fat, lazy, sweet, and loving cat, up the stairs to her apartment. The cat went directly to the door, looking anxiously over her shoulder — it was suppertime, and Sophie, who spent her days down in the shop cadging treats from customers, was determined never to miss any kind of a meal, even the sad pittance of Iams Less Active that Betsy allowed her.

Betsy fed her, changed into casual clothes — jeans and a sweatshirt — then fixed herself a quick salad, did a little housework, and went back down to the shop to open the door to members of a class in black-work that Lisa Hugo was teaching.

A middle-aged, comfortable-looking woman with long salt-and-pepper hair cascading down her back, Lisa doted on the more difficult areas of needlework, particularly Hardanger. She did blackwork for relaxation. She was a patient, competent, experienced teacher.

Blackwork is the thinking stitcher's needlework, she told Betsy and the five women gathered for the class. "You may spend more time thinking about your pattern than stitching it, because you have to think about where to begin, in which direction to go, and how to complete it.

"Blackwork is a form of embroidery, worked on even-weave fabric. It is done in black thread on white fabric if you like, or red on white, or brown on tan, or yellow on navy. It is always reversible — mostly. It is not counted cross-stitch, but counted embroidery, except when you don't do it on even-weave or make it reversible. It is usually recognized by its geometric form.

"But purists like it done in black on white and as a mirror image; that is, the pattern is the same on the front as on the back. It's not magic, but there is some trickery to it.

"It is an extremely old form of needlework, very popular among the Tudor monarchs of England, beginning with Henry the

Eighth, whose first wife, Katherine of Aragon, is said to have brought it to England from Spain — though we now know that isn't true. In 'The Miller's Tale' by Geoffrey Chaucer, who wrote in the late fourteenth century, we find:

> Whit was hir smok, and broyden al
>   bifoore
> And eek bihynde, on hir coler aboute,
> Of col-blak silk, withinne and eek
>   withoute."

So far as Betsy could tell, Lisa's Middle English accent was flawless.

But Lisa saw the puzzled faces looking back at her, and relented. "Let me translate that: 'Her smock was white; embroidery in coal black silk repeated its pattern on the collar front and back, inside and out.' That sounds like a description of blackwork.

"One theory of why blackwork was so popular in the sixteenth century — and it was very popular — is that it looks like lace. Lace was incredibly expensive because just a few knew how to do the long and tedious work of making it. Only people above a certain rank were supposed to wear it — sumptuary laws, you know. Our chief source for fifteenth-century patterns are the portraits of Hans Holbein — most of the fabrics themselves are gone. But Master Holbein was painting portraits of nobility and even royalty, who wore lace as well as blackwork. So it was loved for its own sake.

"Okay, history lesson over. Let's get closer to picking up our needles. Blackwork uses what is called a 'double running stitch.' "

Lisa handed out large squares of natural-color fiddler's cloth, whose weave resembled Aida cloth. It was fourteen count, nice and low to make it easier to follow the pattern they would be stitching on it. She had them practice a double running stitch along one edge, stitching over two in one direction, then coming back to stitch over the under-stitches and under the overstitches, to make a solid line.

"If you turn it over, you will see that same line on the underside — and that, my children, is how blackwork is done."

Lisa had selected as a class project a pincushion in a pattern called Harvest Time. It had a center medallion in a zigzag outline, with vines and a leaf coming off each of the four sides. She held up a pretty little pincushion about three inches across — "We will make two copies of the pattern and stitch it corner to side so it will have eight sides. When you begin using finer weaves, you may want to do this again as a small traveling pincushion — and when you are really advanced, you can do it on fabric with such a high count that you end up with a button." She brought out a tiny padded model barely an inch across. "I've seen stitchers bring these to conventions to trade or give to friends they meet there.

"So, let's get started. You want to pull off three strands of your six-stranded floss . . ."

Surprisingly, the work began not in the center, but with one of the leaves, and stitching that first leaf took a leap of faith, as it didn't look at all like a leaf, but a random series of small stitches around a vague open space.

Betsy lost her way the first time, frogged it, got it wrong again. The third time she got it so wrong that even Lisa couldn't see where the problem was. All she could do was take it out completely and start it from the other direction. The weave of the fabric was so loose, and the three strands of floss so sturdy, she could undo the work as often as necessary without damage to anything but her patience.

The fourth time, coming back along the "random stitches," the leaf became manifest, to Betsy's great satisfaction. Then she worked the two curling vines off the stem of the leaf, making two mistakes in the first one from overconfidence.

The class was to have a second session. Homework after the first was to finish two copies of the pattern. In the next lesson, the students would learn how to stitch it together. Lisa also promised a glimpse of a more advanced kind of blackwork, in which an outline first was stitched on the cloth and then was filled in with "shadowing," or stitching with a repeated geometric pattern.

Covered in the cost of the class was a copy of *Why Call It Blackwork?* by Marion Scoular. "There are dozens and dozens of geometric patterns in that book. You will want to look through it and find one you think would fill a shape you select. The book has a nice outline on the last page — a teacup, teapot, and tea cozy — but you may want one of the simpler ones found in the hand-outs I gave you, or just something you choose yourself. Look around, you'll be surprised at how many pattern outlines are suggested by everyday things."

Betsy, not a fast stitcher when learning something new, had only the first of her two patterns half finished when the class was dismissed.

Blackwork is not magic, Betsy recalled Lisa saying, putting things away. *But it* is *trickery.*

She wished it were magic; she could use a magic wand to convince her brain to easily follow that simple pattern. Blackwork was like Hardanger — which she couldn't get at all — in that the forward stitching must be done correctly, or the backstitching wouldn't come out right.

She wondered if she would find blackwork to be as discouraging a craft as Hardanger. Like the tricky case of murder she was also foundering on.

EIGHT

After the class ended around nine, Betsy felt too restless to go back upstairs for the night. Of course, she had a knitting project to work on, there was bookkeeping to be done, she hadn't checked in with her newsgroups in two or three days, and she needed to put up the new shower curtain she'd bought last week. Plus it was blowing a gale out there in the dark. The wind was driving thin droplets of water hard enough to sting the face of anyone foolish enough to be outdoors.

On the other hand, it would make her feel brave to go out for just a little walk.

She did go back upstairs, but only long enough to put on her oldest walking shoes and her raincoat, a new tan Burberry with a hood. She tied a pink scarf around her neck to keep the hood in place, and drew on leather gloves. She put her wallet in a pocket

144

along with her keys, and set out for Water Street.

Her building was on Lake Street, which ran into Water Street — Excelsior's main thoroughfare — very close to the lake. There were several slips for large cruisers, the kind that could handle a wedding reception on their three decks. Two were tied up, looking forlorn in the dark and shiny wet. Next to the slips was a big wooden wharf.

Betsy caught herself using the word *big* in connection with the wharf, and smiled. Compared to the huge wharves that accommodated seagoing ships in the port of her old home town of San Diego, this wharf was barely big enough to deserve the name. But it was enormous compared to the narrow plank walkways people built out into the lake behind their cottages. Two of the lake cruisers could tie up at the same time to load passengers, with room left over for a couple of motorboats or a sailboat or even one of those twenty-foot yachts that populated the lake in the summer.

But the wharf was unoccupied at present, its wood slick with rain. The lake itself was choppy, with little whitecaps dotting it here and there, gleaming in the streetlights. Far away were the lights of Wayzata, and all along the lakeshore glowed the ample win-

145

dows of the year-round mansions that were replacing the modest summer cottages.

Betsy leaned on a railing and thought dark thoughts. What was the matter with her? She hadn't even begun to sleuth in this case. What was she waiting for? A clue or two to drop out of the sky into her lap? Why wasn't she going around asking questions?

Was it because she was afraid of the answers she might find?

Lisa's casual remark — that blackwork wasn't magic, but trickery — crossed her mind again. That might describe the murder of Ryan McMurphy. Of course, she didn't believe in black magic. What modern person did?

Right?

It wasn't blackwork that killed Ryan, but it was trickery. However, what she needed in his case was not just the method, but the name of the magician.

Betsy leaned on the railing again. She was feeling about as hopeless and incompetent as she had when she first started sleuthing. She hadn't a clue about Ryan's murder — literally. Not one clue.

Lots of people disliked Ryan, and for good reason. While drunk, he was a singularly unlikable person. Jill had told Betsy what she'd heard from Mike Malloy, that the

146

person most likely to have done him in, his wife, had a solid alibi.

So who else was there?

Well, Joey Mitchell was alleged to hate him, because Ryan had spoiled his ambition of a career as a firefighter.

Who else?

Godwin's murmured reply echoed in her mind: Leona Cunningham. But Betsy was sure in her heart that it wasn't Leona.

Right?

Or was she afraid it might be Leona? Was that why she was afraid to get serious about sleuthing?

She sighed and lifted her head to let the wind and rain beat at her face. Perhaps the pummeling would clear her thought processes.

And then there was blackwork. What on earth possessed Betsy to sign up for the course? Her job was to sell the fabric and threads and yarns her customers desired to work their projects, not to sit at a table showing everyone how slow a learner she was. By tomorrow every needleworker in town would know that Betsy couldn't master a simple blackwork pattern. People would come in and laugh at her.

Betsy heaved another heavy sigh. The wind started to blow at a new angle, making the ends of her scarf slap her in the face. She took the scarf off to retie it, when a huge gust of wind snatched it from her hands. It went whirling up the wharf, across the bit of park, and into the street, where a large truck immediately ran over it.

Well, didn't that just put the cherry on top of her evening? It was a good scarf; she'd knit it herself in a cheerful pink wool-cotton-blend yarn. Worse, it was the one where she'd learned a lot of stitches by making a sort of sampler of the thing.

She trudged off the wharf, up the bit of soggy grass, and into the street. The scarf was soaked, of course, and seemed to have picked up a heavy load of road grime as well as an enormous black tire print.

Betsy wrung it out and shoved most of it into a pocket. She set off walking again, holding her hood closed at her throat with one hand. Without really having a goal in mind, she found herself on Oak Street, where Leona lived. Leona's house was on a corner lot, set well back from the street. It was a late Victorian house, sort of Queen Anne style, not really large but with roofs angling off in all directions. She stopped at its front gate. Not a light shone anywhere within it. A wraparound porch seemed less an invitation to call than a device to hide the entry. The lot was large, set with mature trees, edged on three sides by overgrown shrubbery. The front was marked by a tall, wrought-iron fence topped with spikes — *à la* the Addams Family. The trees were mostly leafless now, though one was still shedding, its leaves flying as though running away from something.

The gate was ajar, but for some reason Betsy did not feel like walking up to ring the doorbell or heading around to the back to see if a light was on in the kitchen.

As she turned to walk away, a movement caught her eye. Something — no, someone — was coming along the line of trees leading to the sidewalk where she stood. Whoever it was — a short woman, dressed all in black — kept looking at the house and therefore didn't see Betsy until she stepped onto the sidewalk.

"Irene!" exclaimed Betsy.

The woman started violently, then clutched her black-gloved hands to her breast. "Goodness gracious, Betsy, you frightened me!"

"I meant to! What are you doing sneaking around Leona's yard?"

"I'm not sneaking!"

"Then what are you doing? The house is dark. It's obvious no one's home."

"Well . . . well, someone has to keep an eye on her, you know! I didn't know she wasn't at home! The woman's dangerous — there's no telling what she's getting up to, mixing up potions in her backyard, casting spells hither and yon."

"How long have you been spying on her?"

"Um . . . not long."

"Who put you up to this?"

"No one! It was my very own idea!"

"Well, stop it. If you don't, I'll tell Leona, and she might call the police about it. Lars Larson would adore to arrest you, you know."

Irene turned as white as paper, and gasped twice, but could not manage a reply. Instead, she turned and hurried away.

Betsy watched her go, then realized she'd had enough of braving the dark and rain. She would just go home.

Seeking light, she walked over to Water Street and turned down it. As she came nearer the lake, she saw a bright patch outshining the streetlights and closed shops' night lights. It was a sign, an imitation of the painted boards found outside British pubs. The picture on it was of a sheaf of barley and a spray of hops, arranged like a bouquet in an old wooden barrel with simplified Old English lettering: THE BAR-

150

LEYWINE. It was swaying in the wind, making a faint creaking noise.

She almost walked past, but the light from the big mullioned bay window glowed pale gold, an invitation to escape the chill rainy night. She paused to look inside.

The place had just four customers. The jukebox was showing its rich jewel colors and Betsy could hear, faintly, the big band sound of "Little Brown Jug."

Billie Leslie stood behind the bar. She was smiling and pulling a big white vertical handle that released a stream of beer into a large glass mug.

Billie laughed at something her customer said. Then a movement behind her caught Betsy's eye and she saw there was someone in the microbrewery room behind the glass wall. Leona.

Betsy opened the door, and several people looked around. "Hi, Betsy!" Billie shouted to her, a little louder than necessary over the talk and music. There was a smell of fried meat and potatoes and beer.

"Hi, Billie!" called Betsy. It was all so jolly after the cold, dark outdoors that her spirits lifted immediately. She came to the bar as the jukebox segued smoothly from "Little Brown Jug" to "String of Pearls." "Could I speak to Leona?"

"She's in the brewery. Want me to go get her?"

"Yes — wait, maybe not. I've never seen a microbrewery up close. Would it be all right if I went back there?"

Billie teased, "Are you a responsible adult?"

"I think so."

"Are you drunk?"

Betsy smiled. "No."

"Do you plan to play with the dials and knobs or turn on one of the hoses?"

"No."

"Then go on in." She pointed to a glass door framed in stainless steel.

The customer Billie had just served looked petulant. "You never let me go back in there."

"That's because I suspect you want to see how much beer you can slam down before we catch you at it and toss you out."

"Awwww, Billie! Only a gallon or two!"

Betsy opened the door and was greeted by a strong smell of beer wafting on a chill breeze. She stepped inside quickly and closed the door.

All the noise from the bar was cut off, and in the silence she could hear a stiff-bristled broom scrubbing the floor and another sound, of a little motor. And floating above those noises, an alto voice, singing what sounded like an Appalachian folk song.

I am my mother's savage daughter,
I-will-not-cut-my-hair . . .

Betsy took a step away from the door to peer around the first of a row of three tall stainless steel tanks. In front of the row near the other end was Leona, pushing a slightly sudsy liquid across the red tile floor toward a drain. She was wearing a pair of very elderly twill pants, black Wellingtons, a chambray shirt under a Barleywine apron, and heavy rubber gloves. An odd little machine, sort of like an old-fashioned tank vacuum cleaner on tiny wheels, had a really long red hose hooked up to it somehow. The hose was running into the top of one of the tanks, and liquid was oozing out the bottom. A double handle on the machine had a meter on it with several black knobs and a little green flashing light.

Betsy found she was holding her breath and thought herself a fool for eavesdropping. She let out the breath and knocked hard on the nearest tank.

Leona stopped short, turned, and saw Betsy, who had put on her most harmless quizzical look.

153

"Hey, hello, Betsy," Leona said. "What brings you out on such a night?"

"I'd like to talk with you."

Leona nodded and gestured at an old office chair, pulled up to a very cluttered desk across from the row of tanks. "I'll be finished in a few minutes," she said, "if you want to wait."

"All right." Betsy came closer but did not immediately sit down, as she was still shedding rainwater. "Tell me what you're doing," she requested.

"Cleaning out this tank with a caustic. I'm almost done. Then I'll rinse it good, and do a transfer of wort from that tank over there" — she pointed to a big, squat stainless steel tank at the other end of the brewery near the front window — "to this tank here, and start brewing a new batch. Then I'll check the progress of the beer in this vessel here" — she rapped on the tank next to the one being rinsed — "and then I'll be done."

"How long does it take to make beer?"

"It's eight hours from mash to wort —" Leona saw Betsy's incomprehension and started over. "Mash is what you get when you take roasted sprouted barley, grind it coarsely, and mix it with water. Wort is what you get after you cook the mash and strain the solids out."

Betsy nodded.

"Then it's cooled, yeast and hops are added, and it's put in one of these temperature-controlled fermenting vessels." Leona pointed to the tall tanks beside her. "I can make a good stout in nine days at seventy degrees."

Betsy looked around. "I guess there's a lot more to it than a bucket of water, a bushel of oven-roasted barley, and a handful of yeast."

Leona sighed. "Yes, people think they yearn for the good ol' simple days of home-brewed beer, until they get a mouthful of something really bad." She resumed her sweeping. "Are you here to ask me something specific, or just finding a place to rest out of the rain?"

At that moment, Betsy decided not to tell Leona about Irene spying on her. "Well, a bit of both, I suppose. You've heard about the dead mice in Shelly Donohue's sewing room?"

Leona stopped pushing the broom to lift it one-handed, and lift her shoulders and her eyebrows as well. She nodded all the while, to show she had heard — and heard, and heard. Back when it was the Waterfront Café, her place was the biggest single source of gossip in the community. Apparently its transformation into a brew-pub hadn't changed that aspect of it much.

Betsy laughed.

"I've heard even bugs died of whatever was in that room," Leona said.

Betsy asked, "Any idea what it might have been?"

"I think it was something Ryan brought in there to eat, something poisonous or with poison put into it. He ate enough of it to make him pass out, and the mice and bugs came out and ate what was left and they all died of it."

"But there wasn't a dirty plate or foam box found in the room."

"Plate? *Ryan?* He probably had it in his hand, or his pocket."

"Hmmmmm."

Leona nodded. "I hear the medical examiner is taking another look at whatever he kept of Ryan, and I bet he is going to say there's strychnine or arsenic or maybe something more subtle in his blood." She turned the tank thing off and finished sweeping, then went to hang the broom in a corner.

When she came back to the desk, Betsy said, "Okay, here's the sixty-four-dollar question: Where were you on Sunday night?"

" 'The sixty-four-dollar question'?"

Betsy waved dismissively. "From an old radio show. Goddy loves them, and I keep picking up terms from him. So where were you?"

"What time are we talking about?"

"Ryan was found around noon on Monday, and it was estimated he'd been dead for about eight hours, so that would make it around three a.m."

"Then relax, I have an alibi. I worked here from four to midnight, went home to bed, but at a little after one I got a phone call from my neighbor, Lynn Morepark. By one-fifteen I was sitting on the couch in my living room with two of my neighbor's three children while she took the third one to the emergency room with what turned out to be whooping cough. The two are Wallace and Fredericka, ages nine and seven. We sang camp songs — which I had to teach them — and made s'mores in my fireplace. They didn't fall asleep until nearly half past three, the little darlin's." Leona made a face. "And their mother didn't come get them until four."

"No ghost stories?" Betsy was grinning in relief. Leona had a solid alibi.

"And have them wake from nightmares the rest of the week? Their mother had

157

enough to deal with."

"How's the third kid?"

"Andrew's recovering at home. And Lynn's taking her other two for their shots, which she used to think were unnecessary, as soon as their father gets home from Poughkeepsie."

"Well, thanks, Leona. I'd better be on my way."

"No problem."

As she went back into the pub, Billie called, "You get what you needed?"

"Yes, thanks!" She was nearly to the door when she turned and saw Joey Mitchell in the rearmost booth, his one good hand around a mug of beer. A plate of fries was on the table in front of him.

Betsy made a U-turn and went back to see him. Seated across from him was a man Betsy recognized as Excelsior's fire chief. He looked up as Betsy approached, and nodded and smiled.

Joey looked up and recognized Betsy.

"May I have just a few minutes of your time, Joey?" asked Betsy.

"Take all you want," said the chief. "I've got to get home." He rose, pulled his raincoat off the hook beside the booth, and hurried away.

"Sit down, why don't you?" said Joey,

gesturing at the now-empty seat. "Can I get you a beer?"

"All right," said Betsy. "What's the least bitter kind they make here?"

"Well, earlier in the summer there was a cherry beer that was very sweet. There may be some left."

"Really? There's a beer made from cherries?"

"It's called a lambic, and it's sweet with no hops in it — hops are what give a beer what beer drinkers think is a refreshing bite. There's a monastery in Belgium that still makes lambics flavored with all kinds of fruit."

"I'll try it," said Betsy, and Joey raised his hand, summoning Billie's son, now acting as server. "Do you have any of that cherry lambic?" he asked.

"No, but there's a peach variety," Roger said.

"Bring Ms. Devonshire a mug of it," he said. "And another lager for me."

The lambic came in an orange pottery mug, smooth and almost glittery in its shininess.

Betsy was amazed at the taste. "Why this almost isn't beer!" was her first comment. "It's not bitter at all!"

"That's right. No hops, no bite."

"But it's not at all like a soft drink. Or hard cider."

"No, it's its own thing." The two drank for a thoughtful minute or two, then Joey asked, "What did you want to talk to me about?"

"Ryan McMurphy."

Joey's expression soured and then turned sad. "I'm sorry he's dead."

"Really? From what I've heard about you, that surprises me."

"Still, it's true."

"Did you murder him?"

He looked mordantly amused. "No."

"Do you have any idea who might have done it?"

"I don't think he was murdered at all. I mean, wasn't he in a locked room with other people in the house and one window to the outside that doesn't open?"

"Yes. And we're working on how it might have been done. If I asked you to tell me where you were very early on the Monday morning his body was found, could you tell me?"

"I could, but why should I?"

"Because you were very, very angry with Ryan —"

"You were here the night I came in and saw us sit and drink together."

"You could have gotten him drunk on purpose."

"Now why would I do that?"

"Someone suggested that you were hoping he'd drive drunk, as he's done before, and get into an accident that would cripple him like his drunk driving crippled you."

A slow smile formed. "That sounds like something your buddy Godwin would say."

He couldn't possibly know that — anyone might say that. "I believe you know Goddy said it."

He nodded, sipped his beer. "All right, I might've heard something to that effect."

"Is it true?"

He stared at her, but she was better at the waiting game and only looked calmly back at him. At last he sighed and said, "It might've crossed my mind."

"Or perhaps you had in mind something about a fire."

The silence this time was longer. Much longer. Joey worked for an insurance company. His job was investigating fraud, particularly arson.

He swallowed, but said boldly, "I don't know what you're talking about. There wasn't a fire at Shelly Donohue's house."

"But something like smoke was put into that room. Something that didn't leave a mark on his body or a trace behind. Have you any idea what that might be?"

"No. But smoke does leave traces, all kinds of traces."

"Yes, you know about things like that, don't you? Where were you that Sunday night, say from midnight forward?"

The reality of his smile showed how false the previous ones had been. "You are not going to believe this — but you can check. I was playing chess with an old friend, Paul Marlin, who lives in that senior co-op in Saint Louis Park. It must've lasted until nearly four in the morning."

"What time did it start?"

"I'm not sure — late, though, probably after eleven. He and I went out to dinner at this Asian place he likes, then back to his place to talk. I had Monday off, so I didn't mind that it went late or that the games went long. We played in Paul's apartment. I can give you his phone number so you can check it out. I can't believe you think it might've been me."

"Why couldn't it be you? This kind of murder might be just your style. You know how investigations work, and you know how fraud works. And you hated Ryan."

Joey hesitated, then sighed. "Lord, yes, I hated him. I'm glad he's dead — because

162

now maybe I can stop hating him. If he hadn't died in that basement, I might've killed him. I thought long and hard about doing it. That's why I started making friends with him again, so I could get close to him, maybe find a way to do it." He took a deep drink of his lager. "You would not believe how many ways there are to set fire to a car and make it look like an accident."

He took another, shorter drink. When he set the mug down, he said, "But now I don't have to think about it anymore. I'll just tell myself that I would've backed out. I like my job with Boyson Insurance. Do you believe in karma? If I could have stayed on the job as a fireman, I probably would've had some kind of accident and ruined my arm anyhow."

He turned his mug around on the table, looking at the wet mark it was making.

"So if not you, then who?"

He looked at her for a long few seconds before speaking. "Billie Leslie might've. She hated him."

"*Billie?* Why?"

"Because he spread some wicked gossip about her daughter Cara." He shrugged. "Or at least that's what Ryan told me that last night he was alive. But Ryan isn't very reliable when he's drunk."

Betsy nodded, adding that tidbit to her store of information.

Joey said, "Now Ryan's gone, who's gonna drive that fire truck he fixed up in the parade?"

"I don't know, I haven't heard."

"Can I do it?" He looked up at her. "Please?"

"Can you handle it? Maybe I can arrange for you to ride on it."

"No, I want to drive it. I can rig the steering wheel, put a suicide knob on it. Come on, I'm the one who got the coats for the riders, you guys owe me something."

"Why is this so important to you?"

"Call it a last hurrah for a dead dream. Okay?"

"I'll talk to Billie for you. But you have to go see Ryan's wife — the truck is hers now. Meanwhile, let me ask you this: Did you come into The Barleywine looking for Ryan the night of the meeting?"

"No, I came in for something to eat and he was there. Already drinking, too."

"No, he wasn't. All he had was a Coke. I saw him drinking a Coke. He came over to the table where we were sitting to make his report, and I didn't smell anything on his breath, nor did he act drunk. And anyway,

The Barleywine wouldn't serve him alcohol."

"He wasn't drunk, but he'd been drinking," insisted Joey. "I could smell it on him — hard liquor, not beer, so he must've started before he came in, because they don't serve hard liquor in here. When we'd been sitting there for a little while, he asked me to buy him a beer."

"Just out of the blue sky?" said Betsy.

Joey looked defiant. "All right, I was leaning on him over those damn Cokes. And once he started, I encouraged it."

"Chug-a-lug," said Betsy, remembering now where she'd heard it.

"Yeah, yeah. I thought about offering to drive him home once he had a load on, but he got out ahead of me. I'm glad now. I wasn't then, but now I am."

"All right. Well, I've got to get home. Thank you for talking with me."

He offered the traditional Minnesotan reply, "You bet."

Betsy went out into the storm, thoughtful. She didn't think Joey was lying about the chess game, but he'd started out by lying to her, so who knew? And if Mr. Marlin was really a good friend, he might lie for Joey. She'd pass this along to Mike Malloy to check out.

165

Between the lambic and the walking, she was tired when she got home. She went right to bed, but her sleep was troubled with dreams. The oddest one had her surrounded by running oranges. She picked one up and found it had horses' legs, complete with tiny metal shoes. She was about to pry a horseshoe off with a screwdriver when she woke up to find her cat Sophie touching her worriedly on the shoulder. Had she been giggling in her sleep? Certainly the idea of cantering oranges was silly enough.

In a much better mood, she got up and dressed for work.

NINE

Godwin was at Rafael's place on Saturday afternoon, a spacious apartment carved from an old mansion in the Loring Park neighborhood. There were six units in this building and eight in the one next door, which formed a condominium. Rafael had what were once the front and rear parlors and half the old library. They were now a bedroom and bath, a living room, and a kitchen that was open to the living room. There were lots of windows, high ceilings, and a set of French doors leading out to a small backyard shared by all the tenants. There were pale hardwood floors, beautiful Persian carpets, white plush and white leather furniture trimmed in chrome and ornamented with bright-colored pillows. An electric fireplace was built into a corner. The art on the walls was Mexican impressionist. One of the windows was stained glass, featuring a knight in full armor climb-

167

ing a rocky height, his eyes fastened on the heavens. It was Victorian — the knight had an anachronistic handlebar mustache.

Godwin loved it; he loved the whole place. He was — rarely for him — speechless with admiration.

Rafael, amused and pleased at his friend's reaction, said, "So you will help me at the party tonight?"

"Oh, yes, of course. What do you want me to do?"

"Well, Paul is making hors d'oeuvres, and Doug is mixing drinks. Could I ask you to carry them around to my guests? Oh, and when we start the poetry, I want a spooky effect, so I have bought a washtub at a secondhand store and some dry ice. I want you to make sure there is water and dry ice in the tub, so we will have that, what is it, 'ground fog' effect?"

"Ooooooooh, I think that will be great! Where's the tub? Where do you want to place it?"

They looked around and decided the little coat closet right inside the door was the best place. "We'll have people put their coats on the bed," decided Rafael.

The theme of the party was The Poe Tree, and each guest had to bring a Halloween-themed poem to read while wearing a costume suitable to the poem.

Godwin adored costume parties, but was less sure about poetry. Still, he remembered one verse of a poem the father of a childhood chum used to recite when the subject of ghost stories would come up. He looked the rest up on the Internet and hoped it would do.

His costume was that of a child from the early twentieth century: a Buster Brown suit. It consisted of a red, Russian-style tunic with a stand-up collar and a three-button fastening on his right shoulder, matching shorts, white ankle socks, and black Mary Jane shoes. The costume was topped with a broad-brimmed yellow sailor hat trimmed with a broad red ribbon. A shop appropriately named Licks on Water Street in Excelsior had provided the crowning touch, an enormous striped lollipop. He felt both exhilarated and ridiculous driving over to Rafael's condo in his little sports car, like a child in a toy car. He both hoped no one noticed him, and hoped everyone did and thought his outfit too sweet to be endured.

Rafael wore a black velvet suit with a broad-collared white shirt and enormous floppy tie — he was Edgar Allen Poe — and he kicked off the party by reciting "The

Raven" from memory. Most people are familiar with the opening verse, *Once upon a midnight dreary* . . . But few get as far as the final verse:

And the Raven, never flitting, still is
    sitting, still is sitting
On the pallid bust of Pallas just above my
    chamber door,
And his eyes have all the seeming of a
    demon's that is dreaming,
And the lamplight o'er him streaming
    throws his shadow on the floor;
And my soul from out that shadow that
    lies floating on the floor
Shall be lifted — nevermore!

Rafael's voice was low and thrilling. Godwin sat transfixed through the recital. Then he felt ashamed of his silly poem and went off to the kitchen to refill the tray with drinks while the others commented on the performance.

All of a sudden Rafael was behind him, his voice concerned. "What's the matter? Did you not like it?"

"Oh, Rafael, I *loved* it! But now I think you'll laugh at my little offering."

"Never!" Rafael laughed softly, then caught himself. "If ever I have laughed *at* you, then I swear, 'Nevermore!' Do you understand?"

Godwin took a relieved breath. "All right. But get someone else to go next. I need to get this tray loaded."

"*Mi amigo,* you are a good friend. Thank you."

As Godwin brought the tray to the guests, one of them, dressed as Shakespeare, was standing and saying, *"Double, double, toil and trouble; Fire burn and cauldron bubble."* There were two long verses that went with that chorus. Godwin hadn't known that. *"Fillet of a fenny snake, In the cauldron boil and bake; Eye of newt, and toe of frog . . ."*

Ugh! thought Godwin, handing the drinks around. His feet shuffled through a layer of chilly cloud riffling across the floor. One of the women present had drawn her feet up on a couch to get out of it.

Godwin selected a glass of orange juice and peach schnapps — a fuzzy navel, the drink was called — and sat down to listen to the next performance.

Penny, wearing a cowboy outfit, recited a haunting poem about an oak tree that died of shame when an innocent man was lynched on it:

I feel the rope against my bark,

And the weight of him in my grain.
I feel in the throe of his final woe,
The touch of my own last pain . . .

Lillian, already a little tipsy, said, "Me, me! I have a nice sad one, may I say it next and be done?"

"You may," said Rafael gravely. "But what are you dressed as?"

She was wearing a white filmy gown, un-cinched, and a sparkly golden headdress shaped like a bishop's miter. "I'm a candle, of course! My poem's called 'The Candle's Out,' by Ann Peters." She stood with her eyes closed, and recited, in a mock-scared voice:

Wind is wuthering 'round house wall —
These nights are hard for all —
Life's candle flickering, guttering low,
That a Healer's craft can only stall,
Strong were those arms, now so lax;
Stern were those lips, now in repose.
Illness melting flesh like wax,
Till Death — Grim Healer — Ends these
    woes.
A gust of wind, And Shadows fall.
The candle's out this night and all.

She doffed her headdress, and bowed her head.

A sad silence fell. Godwin, wishing to lighten the mood, screwed his courage to the sticking point, caught Rafael's eye, and nodded.

"Now we'll hear from the little boy," Rafael said. "Who are you supposed to be?"

"Why, I'm Buster Brown, who was a famous comic strip character," he said. He stood, put down his glass, took a lick of his all-day sucker, and announced: " 'Little Orphant Annie,' by James Whitcomb Riley."

Little Orphant Annie's come to our house
    to stay,
An' wash the cups an' saucers up, an'
    brush the crumbs away,
An' shoo the chickens off the porch, an'
    dust the hearth, an' sweep,
An' make the fire, an' bake the bread, an'
    earn her board-an'-keep;
An' all us other childern, when the
    supper-things is done,
We set around the kitchen fire an' has the
    mostest fun
A-list'nin' to the witch-tales 'at Annie tells
    about,
An' the Gobble-uns 'at gits you
Ef you
Don't

Watch
Out!

Wunst they wuz a little boy wouldn't say
    his prayers,
An' when he went to bed at night, away
    up-stairs

The pleased attention Godwin was getting
encouraged him. He'd made his voice high
and childlike. Now he drew out the words
and gestured upward:

A waaaaaaaaay up-stairs . . .
His Mammy heerd him holler, an' his
    Daddy heerd him bawl,
An' when they turn't the kivvers down . . .

Godwin paused for effect, and whispered
the next line with horrified delight:

He wuzn't there at all!
An' they seeked him in the rafter-room,
    an' cubby-hole, an' press,
And seeked him up the chimbly-flue, an'
    ever'wheres, I guess;
But all they ever found was jist his pants
    an' roundabout —
An' the Gobble-uns'll git you
Ef you . . . don't . . . watch . . . out!

174

Huge success! Applause! Godwin took three bows, then had to go to the kitchen and drink half a pint of bottled water to cool off. He was glad he hadn't recited the whole poem — there were two more verses — better always to leave your audience wanting more.

Back in the living room, Dan broke out his button accordion and set off on the sad story of a ghost named Miss Bailey who, after hanging herself, had returned in spectral form to confront the man who drove her to it. But Godwin was still too elated to go back.

Jane was halfway through "The Cremation of Sam McGee" when Godwin noticed that the fog moving restlessly across the floors seemed to be getting a little thin. He put on heavy gloves and took another chunk of dry ice out of the ice chest in the kitchen and slipped quietly over to the front closet to check on the tub.

It was dark over there — Rafael had sought atmosphere by turning the lights down low and setting candles everywhere but in this distant corner — and he couldn't see very well. He bent over. The water was seething, but just barely. Did it need another chunk?

■ ■ ■ ■

Jane finished "The Cremation of Sam Mc-
Gee" by repeating the first verse — *"There
are strange things done in the midnight sun /
By the men who moil for gold . . ."* — in
chorus with several others who knew at least
that part of the poem by heart. There were
cheers and laughter.

"Where's Goddy?" asked someone.

They looked — it took a minute or two —
and found his still form on the floor beside
the open closet door.

Rafael picked him up and carried him to
the couch, where, in a matter of seconds,
Godwin started to wake up.

"Oooooh, my head!" he groaned. "Who
hit me?"

TEN

On Sundays, Betsy always attended the early service at Trinity Episcopal. She found that if she didn't go early, she tended not to go at all.

But eight o'clock on a Sunday morning in October was very early. The sun was just up and the ceremony so familiar it barely stirred her to complete wakefulness.

She was awake enough to give thanks for the prompt rescue of Godwin at Rafael's party last night. "O Lord," she prayed, "keep Your eye on that little sparrow. Thank you."

Jill stopped her on her way out of church. "How's it coming?" she asked.

"Not well. Did you know Joey Mitchell is a liar? I talked to him last night, and I don't know which of his several stories to believe."

Betsy went home in a renewed funk. But breakfast at home was also familiar, and therefore comforting. She had a Sunday routine of a soft-boiled egg and two strips of bacon. Actually, one strip, but Betsy had purchased one of those microwave bacon cookers and discovered that it worked better if she cut her bacon strip in half before draping the pieces over the plastic holder. Though she'd done the trick to herself — more trickery! — it still felt as if she were getting two strips. *How oddly the human brain is constructed!* she concluded; but in this case, good-oh.

She sat down with her bacon and egg, her morning cup of black English tea, and the Sunday paper.

To her surprise, there was a column on witchcraft from a guest editorialist, a clergyman from Texas. Apparently the news of the mysterious death, and rumors of its cause, were reaching far beyond the town.

Charily, she began to read:

"THOU SHALT NOT SUFFER A WITCH TO LIVE!"

Her heart sank. But then the article continued:

When that was written over three thousand years ago, people believed in witches. They believed a person could injure a neighbor, even kill him, with a spell or other occult method.

Modern man does not — or so you would think.

But apparently such beliefs have not died out entirely. The city of Excelsior, Minnesota, is filled with rumors that the unexplained death of one of its citizens was caused by a practitioner of the Wiccan religion. It is shocking and sad to find such superstitions alive and well in twenty-first-century America.

What makes this situation particularly dangerous is that followers of Wicca themselves believe they can injure an enemy with a spell, if only by putting themselves trebly at risk of the same injury.

There was a time when virtually everyone would laugh at such a notion, but that was when this was a Christian nation, one that had cast off not only the superstitions of the Dark Ages but the even more antique rules of the Old Testament.

Yet today, educated people rearrange the furniture in their houses in the belief that doing so can create health, wealth, and good fortune. Others believe distant planets, and even more distant stars, can affect their daily affairs.

Why have so many in our society aban-

179

doned Christ for feng shui, astrology, Wicca, or other beliefs? It's a symptom of an old, old problem: We want to be our own gods. We want our illusions of personal self-sufficiency and power. And we want the benefits of spirituality without the costs of self-discipline, humility, and obedience.

Why does this worldview have such strength in this era of nonbelief? I think we have a new problem: a belief that *there is no ultimate truth,* that the only unforgivable sin is lack of tolerance. But the virtue of tolerance can easily become the sin of relativism. And that means any religion claiming to have a unique, authoritative truth is not only implausible, it is offensive.

If you remove God from a culture, it will seek elsewhere for belief — because despite the efforts of the secularists, man is and will remain a creature of faith. And the faiths he invents can be not only reservoirs of ignorance but a danger to himself and the very culture he depends on to protect him in his beliefs.

Leading, apparently, to the danger of a crowd gathering with torch and pitchfork to march off and execute, without trial, an innocent woman.

Well! thought Betsy, in her best Jack Benny voice. That last shot should offend as many people as possible. Including not just the slack-jawed, unsophisticated denizens of Excelsior but poor, innocent Leona.

The next day, Monday, Betsy turned the shop over to three part-timers. She had given herself several tasks. One was to find a carpenter to repair the long white counter that thrust out from one wall of her shop. A customer had wheeled her baby in to show him off and ran the stroller straight into one of the glass cabinet doors, without injuring the baby, whose vehicle was built in the lines of a tank, but breaking not only the glass but the thin wood stiles that separated it into four panels.

Another was to interview a man who wanted to rent an apartment. Betsy owned the building her shop was in. On the ground floor were her own shop, a secondhand bookstore called ISBN's — currently on its third owner — and a delicatessen famous for its roast beef sandwiches and huge sour pickles.

The second floor was divided into three apartments. Betsy had one; Frank and Joy, a young married couple, lived in another; and Doris Valentine rented the third. Last year Doris's apartment had been burglarized and she nearly moved out, saying the place now held horrid memories. Betsy had decided to renovate the apartment — and so long as she was about it, the young couple's apartment, too.

But now Doris was going to marry Phil Galvin. The wedding was very soon and would be small, a service in the tiny old chapel of Trinity Episcopal Church. "Because it has to be in church," said Phil — surprisingly, because he was not a member of any church. Doris had been raised Catholic but she had wandered through many denominations over the years, with a detour into Buddhism that lasted only a few months. So it was also a surprise when she strongly agreed. She asked Godwin to be her Man of Honor, so Phil asked Betsy to be his Best Woman. Then Phil asked Betsy to find a minister to perform the ceremony, and Betsy was pleased when Father John of Trinity said he'd be honored to do it.

Godwin, meanwhile, had gleefully begun to plan the bride's trousseau, starting with a wedding gown. It took some strenuous talking to get him to see that white taffeta under green chiffon sprinkled with sequins and rhinestones was not going to happen.

Phil had his own house, so naturally he

was taking his bride home to live with him
— and that meant Betsy was out a tenant.

"With the beautiful remodeling you did in
here, you shouldn't have any problem finding a new renter," said Doris.

It started off well. The first day her rental
ad appeared on Craigslist and in the paper,
she got a half dozen calls.

Today she was showing the apartment to
a young man who looked for all the world
like Ichabod Crane. He brought his clingy
girlfriend along to see Doris's one-bedroom
place. What on earth did she, an exceedingly attractive young woman, see in him?
Betsy wondered. As they finished touring
the little apartment, Betsy's other tenants
came to stand in the open door.

Ichabod and Miss Cling said they weren't
sure about the place. "It's kind of small,"
Ichabod noted after his girl whispered in
his ear while casting sly looks at Betsy over
his shoulder. Did she think Betsy might
become a rival for his affections?

As they went out, Betsy's other tenants
said, almost in chorus, "Can we talk to you
for a minute?"

"Sure," Betsy replied. She gave Miss Cling
her card and told them she had more people
interested in seeing the place, so they

shouldn't wait too long to make up their minds.

After they vanished down the stairs, Betsy turned to the couple and said, "Okay, Joy and Frank, what can I do for you?"

"We want to give notice, too."

"Oh, no! Is something wrong?"

Joy smiled shyly and bumped gently against her husband. "Not at all. We're pregnant, and it's with twins, so we'll need a bigger place. Isn't that exciting?"

"Yes, it is, how wonderful for you!"

"We want a yard, too," said Frank, beaming and putting an arm around Joy. "We're having two boys, and they'll need some space to be boys in."

"I'm so pleased for you, congratulations! All right, today's the twenty-fifth, your last day will be November twenty-fourth, all right?"

She went back to her apartment to make a note of their date of departure on her calendar and sat down to write a new ad. "For Rent: Newly renovated second-floor walkup, quiet, less than a block from Lake Minnetonka. On-site laundry room. Small, well-behaved pets welcome. Available November 25." She raised the rent thirty dollars a month — she hadn't raised it on Joy and Frank after the renovation — and gave a phone number and the Crewel World web site. She updated the web site to repeat the ad — there was already one for Doris's apartment — and uploaded an "after" picture she had taken when the renovation was finished.

Then she went down to the laundry room in a corner of the basement and started a load. She caught up on her bookkeeping and her newsgroups, updated her grocery shopping list, went down to move the clothes into the dryer and start a new load, stopped in the shop to see how the part-timers were doing, and went out to continue her investigation.

One reason she had taken the day off was that the elementary schools in the district were out for the day for a teachers' conference, so Shelly — who almost never attended the conferences — was home.

"Who is it?" she called in response to Betsy's knock.

"Me, Betsy."

"Come in!"

As Betsy entered, she found Shelly tossing a lightweight blue Saint Paul Saints blanket over her needlework. "Mike Malloy has a crew down in my sewing room again. This time they're doing a more thorough job of treating it like a crime scene. And they're

185

drinking coffee as fast as I can make it," she added with a little sniff. "I knew I should've bought that big coffeemaker when it was on sale at Target. But usually Harv and I just have two cups apiece in the morning. I think I've made fresh for these guys about five times already. They're running me ragged."

She was talking too fast, and her eyes were too shiny. "Are you all right?" Betsy asked.

Shelly sat like a statue for a few seconds then melted into tears. "No," she said. "I'm not handling this well at all! I'm trying so hard, so hard to be b-brave." She broke down completely.

Betsy led her to the couch and made her sit down. She sat beside her, holding her hands. "Take it easy, Shelly," she soothed. "It's all right, this is a terrible situation."

"My beautiful sewing room! I can't go down there anymore! It's ruined for me! Ruined, ruined!"

"Now, now, that's how you're feeling right now — and it's no wonder. But in a little while you'll change your mind, you'll see." She chafed the backs of Shelly's hands. "Now, pull yourself together. You don't want Harvey to see you like this."

"Oh, Harv's been so wonderful!" sighed Shelly. "He's been my rock, so patient with me. Oh, Betsy, I wish I'd given him a chance back when I knew him in high school! All those wasted years! He is so kind to me, so thoughtful and understanding! I could just cry!" In fact, she did start to cry again, then saw the humor in that and turned it into a strange laugh.

Her dog, a short, blocky black-and-tan type who, judging by her long ears and big feet, had basset hound in her ancestry, came to sniff at her legs and whine softly.

"Oh, Portia, it's all right," said Shelly, and the dog wagged her tail and collapsed at her feet.

"She's so sensitive to my feelings," sighed Shelly fondly. "And she hardly ever barks, except at strangers." She leaned forward to confide, "By his second visit, she was greeting Harv like an old friend, but she'd still like to take a bite out of Mike and company."

"Why don't you let Mike and his crew make their own coffee?" asked Betsy.

"Because I don't want them poking around in my kitchen, the nosy snots."

Betsy smiled, then sobered. "Shelly, you know, I'm sure, that I'm looking into this myself."

Shelly nodded, and then grew serious. "What do you want to ask me?"

"Have you been down in your sewing

room since you found Ryan?"

She lifted her shoulders and shuddered. "It's too awful down there. That business with the mice was just too grotesque. They are supposed to be all cleared out, and the walls are repaired, but it still gives me shivers. I store my projects in there, but I bring things up here to work on. It's difficult, and it's making Harv crazy, but I can't bear to be down there."

"That may be a good thing. I want you to go down there in your mind, the day you found Ryan. Picture it in all the detail you can recall, exactly as it was. This might be important. What did you see down there that was wrong? Besides Ryan's body, of course."

Shelly bowed her head and closed her eyes. Betsy was struck by how handsome she was, her oval face surrounded by all that light brown hair, the thick eyelashes underlining her large eyes, her straight nose and sensitive mouth. Normally mobile, her features became still as she drew into herself, thinking. Betsy could see her eyes moving behind the closed lids as she explored the room in her memory.

But all she said after nearly a minute was, "Nothing."

"Nothing was out of place, no chair pulled

188

away, no window open?"

"The window doesn't open. It's made of glass blocks cemented together."

"What did Ryan have in the room? Where did he keep his clothes, for example?"

"In a suitcase, he had this big suitcase. And a couple of grocery bags for his laundry. That stuff was right where he always left it."

"Did you do his laundry?"

"No, of course not."

"Did he eat with you?"

"Yes, except when he was drunk. Once he started getting drunk, I told him he had to eat out."

"He didn't ever eat in his room?"

"I don't allow food in there! Or any drink besides water. He could eat his supper on the porch or in his car if he brought something home. But he did eat breakfast with us, because he was sober in the mornings."

"Did he ever talk at breakfast about someone who was angry with him?"

"Not that I recall."

"What did you talk about?"

"The usual things. The awful weather we're having. What his girls were doing in school. Harv is designing that new park over in the development in Chanhassen, so we talked about that. Once Ryan showed us a new amulet he'd ordered from a town called Raipur in India — can you imagine? From *India!* I said, 'I don't think it works on pink elephants, Ryan!' "

"What did he say?"

"He said it brought peace. He said he could use some peace. And I will admit, he looked hag-ridden. Oh." She pressed her fingers against her lips. Then she sighed. "Was that politically incorrect?"

"I don't know. I think the term for a senior witch is *crone,* not *hag* — it's one they use themselves. And anyway, I should think he was riding Leona rather than the other way around."

"He was afraid of her."

"Apparently he was afraid of a lot of things."

"Including the dark — oh!"

"What?"

"Every night when he got in, he'd light a candle. The lights in the sewing room are very bright, too bright to sleep with them on, but he was afraid of the dark. I told him he could have a candle so he borrowed my big pottery bread bowl — he was afraid of fire, too, poor fellow — and he had this box of white emergency candles he bought at the grocery store. I had a little candle holder I loaned him, and he'd put it in the bowl and put one of those candles in it. He'd light it and let it burn all night, down to nothing. But his last night on earth he must've gotten over his fear of the dark, or let his fear of fire overcome it, because when we looked around the room, we found the bowl beside the futon and the candle was only halfway burned down."

"Or his murderer blew it out."

"Oh, Betsy! Don't say that! The thought of a stranger in my house . . ." She shuddered.

"You think it wasn't murder? Then what was it?"

"I don't know, I don't know." She rocked back and forth in anxiety.

Betsy pulled a little red spiral notebook from her purse. "Who hated Ryan McMurphy?"

Shelly drew her shoulders up. "No one."

"Shelly, we both know that isn't true."

She sat back on the couch, one of those squashy ones, upholstered in putty-colored corduroy. Her royal blue slacks and top made a pretty contrast with it and with her light hair. But she drew her shoulders in as she wrapped her arms around her upper body in distaste. "An ugly question."

"An ugly crime. And you've heard the talk."

"Leona?"

"I now know she has a good, solid alibi. How about Joey Mitchell?"

"How about him?"

"What do you know about him?"

"Not a whole lot. He had wanted to be a full-time fireman since he was a little kid — our Excelsior firefighters are just part-time volunteers, everyone knows that. There are firefighters all over his family, uncles and cousins and grandfathers."

"Does Harv know him?"

"Not very well. He's never said anything to me about him other than he feels sorry for him because of his arm."

"Did Joey ever visit Ryan here at your house?"

"No."

"Who else hated Ryan? Come on, help me out here, Shelly."

"I'm trying! But all right, let me think." She did, for a long while. Finally, as if she was coming to a decision rather than recalling something, she said, "Well, much as I hate to say this, Ryan's wife, LuLu, has to go on your list."

"LuLu? I thought her name was Luella."

"It is. But her baby sister couldn't say Luella and called her LuLu, and it stuck. Anyway, LuLu was sick to death of Ryan's drunken antics, frightened to death he was going to lose his job, and furious with the chaos he was bringing into the lives of the children. They — Claire and Winnie," she said, playing to the notebook in Betsy's hand — "loved him when he was sober and were scared of him drunk; and they never knew which he'd be when he walked in the door at night. Also . . ." Here Shelly paused to think, and to gather her nerves. "All right, there was a really enormous life insurance policy on him. LuLu shouted at him once when he was on a bender, saying what was she to do if he killed himself while he was drinking? How would they pay for the house, educate the kids? So, still half drunk, mind you, he went out and got this policy for two million dollars."

"Good Lord!" said Betsy. "When was this?"

"Just about six months ago. Maybe a little longer, but I don't think it's been a year. He kept the premiums up on it, too, because he seemed to think it gave him permission to drink."

"Two million dollars," said Betsy. For a woman scared of what might happen, two million dollars could buy a lot of relief.

ELEVEN

Betsy, still desperate to "get a clue" as she left Shelly's house, reflected that a viable suspect would have had to know where Ryan was staying. Not just at Shelly's house, but specifically in her sewing room in the basement.

She sat in her car and thought about it. LuLu knew, of course. Then Betsy had a sudden recollection. Ryan had announced at The Barleywine, on that awful night of the committee meeting, that he was staying with Shelly. Rats, that meant that first the committee members knew, and soon after, the whole town knew. Wait, most of the Monday Bunch already knew his body was found in Shelly's sewing room, so that little item was probably already circulating.

So much for that clue.

Still . . . Betsy wrote down the names of the committee members present. Plus Joey Mitchell, he of the maimed left arm, who wanted to drive the fire engine Ryan had restored.

She reminded herself to let Malloy know about Joey's alibi. Let Mike check it out — Joey didn't seem to be lying or mistaken about the night of the chess games, but perhaps he was. Meanwhile, she, Betsy, would cross him off her list.

Now, who on the committee was angry with Ryan?

She had no idea. Who would know? Betsy remembered the indulgent tone in Billie's voice when she brought the little sandwiches and orange to Ryan's booth.

It was Billie who had encouraged Ryan to finish restoring the antique fire engine for the parade, and invited him to the meeting to report success, and led the cheering when he had a super idea for supplying it with ghostly riders. So she knew him, or at least had been talking with him for some while.

Billie was easy to find and probably willing to talk. The one Betsy didn't know was LuLu — and according to Shelly, LuLu was a suspect. She'd better talk to her next.

The McMurphy home was a modest wood-frame bungalow with a deep front porch whose roof was set on pillars, the top half planks, the bottom stones. The house was freshly painted crayon brown with crayon green trim. Lace curtains edged the windows. Two children's bicycles were on the porch, the smaller one pink, with training wheels.

Betsy, weighty with pity for the ugly event that had damaged and possibly destroyed this scene of domestic bliss, went up to ring the doorbell.

Luella — LuLu — McMurphy was pounds lighter than Betsy remembered from seeing her at church. She was tall for a woman, attractive, with naturally curly brown hair cropped short, and hazel-brown eyes. She was wearing deep blue slacks, a black sweater, and a big green apron with autumn leaves appliquéd all over it. Her face was pale, and there were shadows around her eyes, so intense they looked like bruises. Her full mouth was pulled tight.

"Yes?" she said in a very crisp voice.

"Mrs. McMurphy, I'm Betsy Devonshire. I own Crewel World over on Lake Street, but I'm here because I'm looking into your husband's death."

LuLu frowned at her in forming anger, then her brow cleared. "Oh. Yes, I've heard about you doing that." There was a thoughtful silence of about fifteen seconds, which Betsy did not break, before LuLu said, "Very well. Come in."

It was nearly noon, and a little girl could be heard crooning in the kitchen. "Ohhhh-hhh, 'mato soup, ohhhhhhh, crackers, ohh-hhhhh, 'mato souuuuuuuup! Mommy?"

"Yes, darling?"

"Am I finished?"

"Not yet, darling. Mommy has company, can you sit quietly for a little while?"

"Yes, Mommy. I'm eating. Ohhhhhhh, 'mato soup . . ."

"She could do a commercial," said Betsy.

Lulu smiled thinly. "Yes, I suppose she could. Will you have a seat?" She gestured toward a comfortable easy chair upholstered in worn chintz, and she took a matching one, which swiveled to face it. The living room was longer than wide, comfortable and lived in, fully carpeted, with couch, coffee table, fireplace, television, none of it new but all clean and well cared for.

Betsy sat but did not get out the intimidating notebook just yet.

"First," she said, "let me offer my most profound condolences on the death of your husband. It must have been a terrible shock to you."

LuLu nodded stiffly. "It was. I knew he was drinking too much, but I didn't think the damage at this stage was fatal, not yet. I hoped — I'd hoped that making him leave

197

our home would shock him into changing his behavior."

"Shelly told me that she thought it had, that he immediately stopped drinking — but he started in again last week."

LuLu nodded. "Yes, he tried to come into our home drunk, crying and saying he was sorry . . . he was so sorry . . ." She began to cry.

Betsy immediately rose and went to her, stooping to reach for her hands. "This is too hard for you. Do you want me to go?"

"No, no, I want to help you believe this was some kind of terrible accident, not . . . not a murder." She sniffed, and Betsy released her hands so she could reach into her purse and find a Kleenex. LuLu wiped her eyes, blew her nose, and put the Kleenex into her apron pocket.

Betsy asked, "Why do you think it was an accident?"

"Because the room was locked! How could someone asleep in a locked room be killed? It's ridiculous! And anyway, there was an, an . . . autopsy!" She choked to a stop and had to close her eyes while she hid away any unpleasant knowledge of what an autopsy entailed. "The medical examiner said he died of natural causes. Do you know there is a rumor that Leona Cunningham did it with black magic? Can you believe it? This is the twenty-first century and there are people who want to bring back the ducking stool and the stake! It's nonsense! Stupid, scary *nonsense!*"

"I agree," said Betsy firmly. "I completely agree. That's why I'm investigating. I want to prove it's nonsense. Will you help me?"

"How can I help?"

"Answer some questions — perhaps some hurtful, embarrassing questions."

LuLu's big, dark eyes searched Betsy's. "All right," she said.

"Is it true that Ryan took out a very large life insurance policy on his life a few months ago?"

"Oh, you think *I* — well, I suppose you would, if you're looking at murder. Though I hope you aren't too serious about it. Still . . . Anyway, it was more like a year ago. Well, almost a year. Ten — nine months, actually." She seemed a little surprised that it was so recent.

"Is it true that you suggested he do this?"

"No, not exactly. That is, I, uh, well . . . we were having a fight. Another fight, one in a long series of them. And I said his drinking was going to kill him, either from liver failure or a car accident, and what were the children and I to do, since we don't have any savings? And he said not to worry, and a week later he came home with the policy. As if that fixed everything."

She bowed her head and said, so softly Betsy had to lean close to hear, "He wasn't a bad man. When he was sober, he was the best husband in the world. He was sweet and hardworking and he loved me and the kids. And I loved him. Alcoholism is a disease and it was killing him — it did kill him. There was no need for anyone to murder him; he was murdering himself."

"Where were you the night he was killed?"

"Here. Right here. With the girls. Winnie's too young to remember what happened which night, but Claire — she's nearly eight — she's at school, she could tell you we all three slept in Mommy and Daddy's big bed that night, just like we did the previous nights. And ever since, too. Every night since he moved out."

"Mommy?"

They both looked around to see a little girl in red flannel trousers and bright yellow shirt with red teddy bears on it. She was barefoot, and her dark hair was tousled. Betsy guessed the soup had come after a nap.

"Hello, darling."

"Who's that lady?"

"Her name is Betsy Devonshire," said LuLu.

Betsy stood, and the child came to offer her rather grubby hand. She had a tomato soup mustache.

"How do you do, Betsy Dove-sheer."

"That's Devonshire, darling," said LuLu.

"Devon-sheer. Okay."

Betsy took the proffered hand, then stooped. "How do you do? What's your name?"

"Winnie. But *not* The Pooh."

"No, you don't look much like a Pooh Bear, but you do look like a very pretty little girl. I'm very glad to meet you, Winnie. How old are you?"

"I'm three going on four."

"Going on four? That's means you're getting to be a big girl. Are you going to sleep in your own bed tonight?"

"No! I sleep wiff Claire and Mommy every night in the big bed." She gestured widely to show how big it was.

Betsy nodded, satisfied. "I bet that's fun. But I can't stay and talk any more. I must go away now." Betsy straightened and said to LuLu, "May I call on you again if I have more questions?"

"Yes, of course. I wish you luck in your sleuthing."

■ ■ ■ ■

Outside, she checked her watch. Nearly twelve noon. She wanted to be back at Crewel World in time for the Monday Bunch meeting at two. There was enough time to get to The Barleywine and have a quick lunch while she talked to Billie.

Betsy drove over to the brew-pub and found a depressing paucity of customers — and no Billie. From behind the bar, Leona said, "She's gone to Saint Paul to pick up kitchen supplies — there's a special price but only if we send someone over right now. She'll be back in an hour or so."

Betsy used her cell to call Shelly and found out Harvey was in Chanhassen, supervising the cleanup on the park he'd been designing. She had Leona pack up a ham on rye with Swiss, a handful of potato chips, and a long spear of pickle, and set out.

Chanhassen was a pretty and growing town, famous for its dinner theater. The new park bordered a new town house development on the north side of town. Betsy pulled into a freshly tarred parking lot, prepared to eat her sandwich in her car before setting out on a search, but saw four men sitting at a picnic table under a shelter a few dozen yards away. One was a young man in a business suit and raincoat, two were workmen in gray coveralls and muddy boots, and one was wearing jeans, a blue shirt and tie, a tweed jacket, and less-muddy workboots. They were consulting a large sheet of paper that wanted to roll up at the edges.

Betsy got out of her car and started up a freshly graveled walk toward them. As she got nearer, she caught fragments of their conversation, which included terms like *barm* and *punch list.*

"Very good, Mr. Fogelman," said the man in the business suit, and everyone stood. Harvey Fogelman — the one in the tweed jacket — rolled up the big sheet of paper and nodded at the workmen, who turned and walked off. The businessman shook Harvey's hand and came up the walk toward Betsy, giving her a curious glance as he passed by.

The air was chilly, a weak sun unable to warm it. The shelter was a blue-shingled roof set on concrete pillars. Harvey watched the businessman — no, he must be a politician, thought Betsy, here to approve the completion of the park.

She saw Harvey turn to go in the opposite

direction, and hailed him. "Mr. Fogelman! Hold on just a minute!"

He turned to look at her, his face puzzled. "May I help you?" he asked as she came under the shelter's roof.

"I sure hope so," she said, a little breathless from hurrying. "I'm Betsy Devonshire, from Excelsior, and I own Crewel World."

"Oh?" he said. Then his face cleared. "Oh, yes, you're the amateur detective, and a friend of Shelly's." Then the frown came back. "And you want to talk to me about Ryan."

"Yessir, I do. Do you have just a few minutes?"

He considered this for several long seconds, then sighed. "If you'll let me smoke while we talk, okay." He reached into his jacket pocket and produced a pipe and a pouch of tobacco.

Betsy didn't mind the smell of pipe tobacco, and anyway there was a soft breeze flowing under the wall-less shelter. "All right," she said.

He shoved his pipe into the pouch and began some twiddling motion to fill it while she asked, "How long did you know Ryan Mitchell?"

"More years than I'd like to admit."

"How did you meet?"

He stuck the pipe in his mouth, found a lighter in a dungaree pocket, turned it sideways to light it, and sucked its flame into the bowl of his pipe. He took a few puffs to get it going, then said, "After I got out of the service, I fooled around doing groundskeeping and managing a garden center before I decided to get serious about making a career of garden design. So I was sixteen years older than Ryan when we met in technical school. He was taking engine repair and small business management, I was studying garden architecture and small business management. I'm not sure why we hit it off at the start, our ages and back-grounds were so different. But we did have the same dumb sense of humor, and the same taste in music — and women, too. Plus, we were about equally broke. But I had my GI bill to help with school, plus a job, and he only had a job, so I let him share my apartment for less than half the rent, if he'd do more than his share of cleaning up. And he did. He was very cheerful about it, too, even if he did put on a 'Yeth, Mathter' accent when I'd remind him of a chore." He smiled and blew a long streamer of fragrant smoke.

Betsy chuckled. She'd gotten out her notebook and now she made a little note.

"Did you graduate the same year?"

"No, I finished up a year ahead of him, got a job after only two months of looking. He had a job waiting for him. He'd already been working in the engine repair section of the car dealership part-time, and just went to full time. He was really, really good with his hands."

"Was he drinking back then?"

Harvey's face went sad. "I don't think I realized at the time just how much he was drinking. We both used to party pretty heavy when we partied, but it was an occasional thing. Looking back, I think it was more because we couldn't afford it than because he didn't want to get drunk more often. Even back then, he was an ugly drunk, and that's why I decided not to renew the lease on the apartment when it ran out. I didn't have the heart to throw him out, so I told him the landlord didn't want us there anymore, and I found a place with only one bedroom." He puffed on his pipe for a while, but Betsy waited and at last he said, more softly, "He slept on my couch for about a month before he moved in with someone else."

"So why did you invite him to stay with you and Shelly after his wife threw him out?"

Harvey's drawing on his pipe made his hesitation barely noticeable. "Because he really needed a place to stay. He swore he'd quit drinking and he said it would only be a short stay, that he'd talk LuLu into taking him back."

"But when he started drinking again, you didn't tell him to leave."

Harvey's hesitation was longer this time. "I know." He sighed. "I know," he repeated. "I thought Shelly was going to throw us both out — she might've if . . . if what happened hadn't happened. I don't know what I would've done if she threw me out. God, what a mess! I feel so bad for her! She was so angry with him — mostly on LuLu's behalf, but still. Then walking into *that* in her sewing room, that was really unfair. And now hearing it might be murder. I can't believe it! Who could do such a thing?" He seemed to catch himself then, stopping short and swallowing whatever else he was going to say, puffing angrily on his pipe.

Betsy said, "You said yourself Ryan was an ugly drunk. Maybe he hurt someone badly while he was drunk, or threatened to do violence to someone. It could even have been just words. You know, blackmail. He was a friend of yours — had he been boasting about hurting someone in some way?"

Harvey checked his watch and got to his feet in one swift motion. "Not that I can recall. What does it matter? Whatever the threat, it's not there anymore. It's all over, done and over." He knocked the dottle out of his pipe on the edge of the table, ground it into the cement floor with a heavy boot, and put the pipe back in its pocket. "I've got to get back to work. Sorry I couldn't be of more help."

He walked away, leaving Betsy to stare thoughtfully after him.

TWELVE

"I'm *serious!* I would have *died* right there at the party if they hadn't found me in another *minute!*" Godwin alternated between fear and amusement as he told his story to the Monday Bunch.

"You mean to tell us," said Bershada in a doubtful voice, "that that foggy stuff you make with dry ice and water is *poisonous?*" She and three others were sitting at the library table on Monday afternoon. Turnout for the regular meeting of stitchers was thin because there was a very noisy thunderstorm going on outside.

"No-o-o," drawled Godwin. "That is, not exactly. You can breathe it like air, but it doesn't work like air. Your lungs can't get any oxygen out of it. And it gives you a huge headache. I actually thought someone hit me." He touched a place on the back of his head. "Right here."

"I've heard of that," said Emily, surprising

them. When they looked at her, she blushed and said, "You know, you sit in your car in the garage with the door down, and it can kill you."

"Honey, that's carbon *mon*oxide. Dry ice is carbon *di*oxide."

"That's right," said tall, blond Jill, who had not only come out in such frightful weather, but had brought little Erik along. He lay asleep in his carrier on the floor beside her feet. He had slept on the way over, too. Erik could sleep through loud noises so tranquilly his mother at one time thought he might be deaf.

She continued, "Carbon monoxide replaces the oxygen in the blood, so the victim's dark venous blood turns bright red, as he suffocates at a cellular level."

"Jill, honestly —" began Betsy, never a fan of gory details.

"All right, but it's not the same as carbon dioxide poisoning, which is basically suffocation. Dry ice is frozen carbon dioxide. It's heavier than air, and that's why the vapors you make by putting it in water flow across the floor. It's not dangerous unless you fill a whole room with it, which is hard to do because you'd need a practically airtight room to do that."

"Or unless you put your face right down

210

into it," amended Godwin.

"Or unless," agreed Jill placidly. "Which I don't imagine you'll do again."

"Wedding plans all finished?" asked Alice, trying to change the subject. She had had enough of the dangers of frozen carbon dioxide. Mere rain couldn't keep Alice away from the Monday Bunch's regular meetings. Though elderly, she was almost impervious to weather. "I'm not made of sugar," she was inclined to say. "I won't melt in the rain." She loved weddings, and attended many, but she was shy, always sat in the back, and left as soon as the ceremony was over.

"We're ready," said Godwin, as if speaking of a coming battle. A growl of thunder punctuated his words. Godwin looked at Betsy and asked accusingly, "Have you got the rings?" As Best Woman, that was one of Betsy's responsibilities.

"Not on me!" protested Betsy, afraid he was going to ask her to produce them. "But I've put them in the purse I'm going to carry."

"You're not carrying a *purse!*" exclaimed Godwin.

"Of course I am, my dress doesn't have a pocket. It's just a tiny thing, it hangs from my wrist by a thin silver chain. It's all right,

I can have one. You're the one who has to hold the bride's bouquet while she takes her vows."

"Oh, yes, that's right." Godwin began to look dreamy and the women looked at one another and smiled.

"What time do you want us at the church tomorrow?" asked Emily. "The service is at ten, right?"

"Yes. Don't come before nine-forty, please. There are only going to be about twenty of us gathered."

It had started out to be a half dozen, but quickly grew to a dozen, and now was up to twenty-two. Any more and the service would have to be moved from the tiny stone chapel that was Excelsior's oldest church to the big church on the other side of the church hall.

If Phil and Doris had had their way, it would have been four people gathered in Father Rettger's study for three or four minutes followed by lunch at Antiquity Rose.

Instead, under Godwin's prodding, there was to be a complete marriage service down to the throwing of the bouquet outside on the steps. Godwin was inclined to weep with sentiment when he thought about it.

Alice said, "I was hoping Phil and Doris would be here today. I have something for her, something she should have before the wedding." She bent sideways and lifted her big old sewing bag onto the table. From it she pulled a white box about eighteen inches long by a foot wide and not quite three inches deep. It was tied with a pale blue silk ribbon.

"Oh, Alice, can we see it?" cried Godwin, coming around the table to look at the box. "Please, please? What is it?"

She turned her bluff old face to him, prepared to say no, so he shifted tactics. "Is it for the wedding? It is, isn't it? Because you want her to have it now. Well, I'm the wedding coordinator, I'm making all the arrangements, so I just have to see it." He sat down beside her and put a tentative hand on the box. "Please?"

She studied him briefly, while he put on his most beguiling face.

"Oh, you," she said. She pulled at the bow and it came open. She lifted the lid to expose a layer of tissue paper, which she parted with large, gentle hands. Inside was a layer of lace. Two layers. No, three.

Betsy came for a look. "What is it?" she asked. "Oh, Alice, it's bobbin lace!" Years ago Alice had been a well-known maker of gorgeous bobbin lace. She'd had to give it up when her eyes got too old to see the tiny pattern of knots.

"Yes, it's from my collection. I put together ten lengths of it to make this." She held it up. It was a mantilla or headscarf, a gossamer thing of pale ecru, fifteen inches wide and almost fifty inches long. It was made in inch-and-a-half-wide stripes, with tiny hearts in the central band that ran the length of the thing.

"Wow!" said Godwin, testing its near-nothing heft with both hands, turning and twisting and bending to look at it from all angles.

"Ohhhhhh," breathed Betsy, coming to touch the thing very gently with a forefinger. "Perfect, this will be the perfect something borrowed."

"More likely the something old," said Godwin. "Could something for the bride be old and borrowed both?"

"Only old," said Alice. "It's a gift."

"Alice, do you mean that?" asked Betsy.

"I can't believe you want to part with something that lovely," said Jill.

"But I do," said Alice. "Doris has been a good friend to me, and what else am I to do with things like this? I have no family to leave my lace to. And I certainly can't wear something like this." She smiled. "I can just see it over that red hair of hers, though.

Won't it be lovely?"

Godwin threw his arms around her. "You are the *best,* the very *best!*"

Emily said, "But will it go with what she's wearing? Goddy, you've been keeping her wedding dress a big secret, so will this look okay?"

"It will look *fabulous.*" He could no longer forbear talking about it and said all in a rush, "She's going to be wearing a cream wool suit, with tan shoes. Betsy and I are going to wear navy, and Phil will wear his good brown pinstripe — it's in the same color stream as Doris's cream colors. This ecru mantilla will set the whole thing off just beautifully."

Jill said, "Alice, I can't believe you're giving this away. It is simply breathtaking. Are you absolutely sure you don't want it back?"

"I agree it came out very nice, but the newest pieces have been sitting in my cedar chest for at least a dozen years. I have more pieces than these, so it's not as if I'm giving it all away. It was fun choosing the lace that could make something nice for my friend. Bobbin lace looks fragile, but this probably will outlast everyone in the room — even little Erik down there, so sound asleep, the little sweetheart. It's nice to have my lace out of storage, to know it will have its day in the sun." Alice's voice was soft, the expression on her weathered face kind and happy.

"Thank you for saying that!" said Godwin. "Now the sun just has to shine!"

"I think it's wonderful of you to do this," said Betsy. "I'm sure Doris will be pleased to have it. Who gets to take it to her, me or Goddy?"

"Why, I do, of course," said Alice, folding it very carefully back into the tissue paper and laying it gently back in the box. "I'll tell her that her marriage coordinator approves of her wearing it, all right?"

She suited action to words, rising to put on an ancient pair of rubbers, a voluminous raincoat, and taking up a big old bumbershoot before heading out into the storm.

Jill said, "A grand old lady, isn't she?"

Emily said, "Goddy, what else went on at that party you went to?"

The women went back to their stitching while Godwin beguiled them with stories of the great food and drink, the wonderful recitations. He made them shiver with his, "The candle's out this night and all."

"The candle's out," repeated Jill, storing the image away in her sometimes-depressive Scandinavian mind. Betsy was reminded that in medieval symbology, a snuffed candle represented the newly deceased. She frowned over that thought — was it significant? — but then Godwin went merrily into a description of Miss Bailey's request for a bribe for the sexton so she could have a proper burial.

Betsy surprised Godwin by knowing the sad reason for the unfortunate ghost's need. "Suicides couldn't be buried in the sacred ground of a cemetery, as they were considered damned souls," she said. "I remember looking it up after the Kingston Trio sang it in a concert I went to." She sang in a falsetto voice, " 'Bless you, wicked Captain Smith, remember poor Miss Bailey!' "

The door made its two-note announcement of a customer coming in, and Betsy went to serve her — it was Shelly, who must have come directly from the classroom. "I need some new needles, Betsy," she said. "Most of my old ones have rust spots on them."

"Oh, that's too bad! How did it happen? Is that basement sewing room damp?"

"Not at all, I can't understand what happened. Here, look at this." She opened her purse and brought out a little gray plastic needle safe. She unsnapped the catch to expose a white magnetic surface on which were captured six needles. Their silvery smoothness was marred by tiny flecks of rust.

"They look as if they were left out in the rain," remarked Betsy.

Godwin and Emily came over for a look and agreed the needles must have gotten wet somehow. Shelly denied again her basement room was damp. She insisted to Emily that she would have noticed if there had been a flood. No, the water heater and washing machine in the other part of the basement hadn't suffered a broken pipe. And no, it wasn't dew sneaking in a window — the window in the room was filled with glass blocks and did not open. Nor was it improperly installed, so there were no leaks. "That room is dry as the Sahara in August," declared Shelly.

Godwin and Emily declared themselves baffled and went back to their seats.

"Are all your needles rusted like this?" asked Betsy.

"No, only the ones not put away in needle cases. These, for instance, and two left tucked into the corner of works in progress. Those last two left rust marks on the fabric. So I'll need a bottle of Whink, too." Whink was a product that made rust stains disappear as if by magic.

"Not —" Betsy cut herself short with a

glance at the Monday Bunch.

"No, that piece was sitting out on my desk, but there wasn't a needle stuck in it, so it's fine." Shelly smiled. "It's nearly done. I'll bring it in to be finished in a few days."

"Good."

Seeing they weren't going to get any good clues about Shelly's designer piece, the Monday Bunch adjourned their meeting and departed.

Besides the Whink, Shelly bought nearly two dozen needles in various sizes. Not that many were marred by rust, but the needles came in packs of four or six or eight, and besides, once started, it's hard for a needle-worker to stop buying needles. Shelly bought a packet of size 17F Bodkins, two sizes of Chenille, size one and size five Crewel Sharps, and four sizes of Tapestry, from eighteens to twenty-eights.

"The eyes are nearly worn through on my sharps anyhow," she said. "I just don't understand how the others got rusty in the first place. That room has always been almost too dry for comfort. I think it's all the lights in there."

"Can't you give us a hint about the pattern you're designing?" asked Godwin.

"No, not one word. Except I think you'll like it."

219

She would have left then, but Betsy said, "Shelly, may I ask you something?"

"Sure, anything at all."

"Harvey and Ryan were good friends, but I'm sure Ryan's drinking, especially after he tried so hard to quit, was a source of frustration to Harvey."

"If you're going to ask me why I didn't throw them both out, all I can say is that I don't know." She stopped short, cast her eyes toward the ceiling, and sighed. "No, that's not true. I am hopelessly, madly, crazy in love with Harvey. I think he's been trying to ask me to marry him for the past few weeks, but something's stopping him. I had the insane notion that somehow Ryan was preventing him from proposing, but now Ryan's gone, and it still hasn't happened."

"Did Ryan ever say anything to make you think that?"

She thought briefly. "No. And since Harvey's still holding off — he's looking for something or waiting for someone, I'm sure of it. I thought it had to do with Ryan, but I guess it wasn't Ryan after all."

THIRTEEN

As Godwin predicted, the wedding day dawned clear and warm. "Indian summer at last," noted Alice as Betsy and Godwin waited at the top of the steps leading to the old stone chapel on Second Street to greet the guests.

"Dearly Beloved," began Father John a few minutes later in his gentle voice, making the old words sound as fresh as the morning, "we have come together in the presence of God to witness and bless the joining together of this man and this woman in Holy Matrimony."

The congregation sighed, because they were unsophisticated enough to appreciate the familiar old words. They had come not to smirk at the old folks' faltering pretense of love, but to witness a marriage that was, in their considered opinion, beautifully right.

Father John asked, "Doris, will you have

this man to be your husband, to live together in the covenant of marriage? Will you love and comfort him, honor and keep him, in sickness and in health, and, forsaking all others, be faithful to him as long as you both shall live?"

"I will," said Doris.

Phil was pleased to have Doris under the same conditions.

John asked the gathering if they, as witnesses to these promises, would do all in their power to uphold these two persons in their marriage. They said in strong unison, smiling all the while, "We will!"

The first reading surprised no one: First Corinthians ("But the greatest of these is love.") The second, though, was startling:

"A reading from Psalm Eighteen," Betsy announced, "verses four through fifteen, forty-eight and forty-nine."

The breakers of death rolled over me, and the torrents of oblivion made me afraid. The cords of hell entangled me, and the snares of death were set for me. I called upon the Lord in my distress, and cried out to my God for help. He heard my voice from his heavenly dwelling, my cry of anguish came to his ears.

By now the members of the congregation were staring at one another in puzzlement, but Phil reached for Doris's hands and clasped them firmly. They were remembering a dark winter night of mortal danger, when a man armed with a revolver set out to murder them. Betsy had been there, and Lars; they were remembering, too. Godwin and Jill had heard the story; they were listening solemnly. Father John had been told why this reading was chosen, and his expression was one of Christian forbearance. Members of the Monday Bunch gradually realized the context of the reading and they began to smile as Betsy continued to read.

The earth reeled and rocked, the roots of the mountains shook, they reeled because of his anger.

And because Doris had the presence of mind to unleash the power of Lars's Stanley Steamer automobile.

Smoke rose from his nostrils and a consuming fire out of his mouth; hot burning coals blazed forth from him. He parted the heavens and came down with a storm cloud under his feet. He mounted on cherubim and flew, he swooped on the wings of the wind. He wrapped darkness about him; he made dark waters and thick clouds his pavilion. From the brightness of his presence, through the clouds, burst hailstones and coals of fire. The Lord thundered out of heaven, the Most High uttered his voice. He loosed his arrows and scattered them; he hurled thunderbolts and routed them.

Well, perhaps not as awesome as all that, but startling and scary all the same to an unprepared villain.

You rescued me from the fury of my enemies; you exalted me above those who rose against me; you saved me from my deadly foe. Therefore will I extol you among the nations, O Lord, and sing praises to your Name.

Betsy smiled and closed the book. "The Word of the Lord," she said, the ritual ending of a reading.

Then Phil kept hold of Doris's right hand, and invoking the Name of God, he took the rest of her, too "From this day forward, for better for worse, for richer and poorer" — by now his old man's voice was choking, and Doris had tears in her eyes, but they soldiered on — "in sickness and in health, to love and to cherish until we are parted by death. This is my solemn vow."

Then Doris took Phil as well.

Betsy found the rings in her tiny purse, and gave them to John to bless. Doris in her turn said, ". . . and with all that I am, and all that I have, I honor you . . ." as she put onto Phil's finger the mate to the one now gleaming on her own fourth finger.

Then John blessed the couple: "By the power of the Holy Spirit, pour out the abundance of your blessing upon this man and this woman. Defend them from every enemy. Lead them into all peace. Let their love for one another be a seal upon their hearts, a mantle about their shoulders, and a crown upon their foreheads. Bless them in their work and in their companionship; in their sleeping and in their waking; in their joys and in their sorrows . . ."

The tiny electric organ in the chapel had rarely rung the chords so loudly and sincerely as it provided a lift to the feet of the newlyweds as they left.

Godwin caught the bouquet. He was as embarrassed as he was thrilled, and immediately handed it to Betsy. Betsy gave it to Alice, who took it home and kept it for a long time.

FOURTEEN

Over a light supper that evening, Betsy remembered how happy Phil and Doris looked at the service earlier. *What a lovely thing to be in love,* she thought. *Maybe it's not too late for me, either.*

She washed her dishes and then sat down in her comfortable upholstered chair with its angled light shining over her left shoulder and got out her blackwork piece. As sometimes happened, her brain fought against the new kind of pattern, then suddenly surrendered. In another few minutes she was enjoying following the kinks and jogs of the twining pattern. As that happened, the rhythm and repetitions soothed her troubled mind and allowed her sleuthing instincts to kick in.

She had a hunch that the solution to this case was staring her in the face, if only she could discern it. She was nearly halfway done with the second blackwork pattern before a glimmer came to her. Two glimmers. She put down her stitching and went first to her kitchen to look for and find the box of white emergency candles she kept there. She set one into a holder and lit it, then carried it with her to her computer, where she logged on to the Internet.

She was surprised by the number of vital record sites for Hennepin County, and disappointed that most of them wanted her to subscribe for a modest fee. Finally, she found a free one linked to the public library and quickly discovered a record of marriage between Harvey Raymond Fogelman and Melissa Jean Brooks. The marriage was recorded twenty-nine years ago — but there was no record of a divorce.

Of course they might have moved away and divorced . . . No, wait, Shelly had remarked one day that Harvey was born in Hennepin County and was determined to die here, never having lived anywhere else. She had said he jested that the reason he went into landscape architecture was because, since he planned on living here all his life, he might as well make it look nice.

So was it possible that Harvey was still married to Melissa?

Betsy sat back in her chair. What had she said to Harvey that spooked him the other day? Something about Ryan threatening violence? Yes, and she had also asked him if it was possible that Ryan was blackmailing someone. Harvey had immediately jumped to his feet and said that whatever it was, it was over and done with, and he had to get back to work.

Had Ryan known or found out that Harvey was still married? If so, when he needed a place to stay and came to ask Harvey to get Shelly to let him move in, had he used that piece of information as leverage? After all, he planned to stay just temporarily. The threat might have been made lightly; perhaps Harvey saw no real harm in it, until Ryan started drinking again. Then his presence would have become much more troublesome. Ryan was, Shelly had reported, a snoop and a gossip. When drunk, and loaded with dangerous information, he was a clear and present danger to Harvey's relationship with Shelly.

So, if her instincts were correct, why didn't Harvey just tell Shelly that he was still married? And why didn't he file for divorce from Melissa Jean?

Betsy set that puzzle aside to do a little work on the second glimmer.

The candle burned at a rate of an inch an hour.

On her lunch break the next day, Betsy drove into Minneapolis and found Metro Ice in its factory-like building off Lyndale Avenue, as she had discovered on the Internet last night. Because they were wholesalers, they would not sell her less than one whole bag of dry ice pellets, which turned out to weigh about ten pounds.

"Leave your window cracked on your drive home," advised the man who sold it to her. "It evaporates faster in pellet form." He put it into another plastic bag, but then punched holes in the plastic with a ballpoint pen. "It swells up and bursts if it isn't vented," he explained.

The pellets were about the size and shape of goose droppings, an unpleasant thought — but that wasn't why Betsy carried the bag well away from her out to the parking lot. It was smoking with cold, and that made her nervous. She put the bag onto the front seat beside her in her car, and drove back to Excelsior with her front windows open a generous two inches. Because the air was filled with a fine drizzle, she arrived back in Excelsior with damp hair.

When she got back to the shop, she found that Leona and Detective Sergeant Mike Malloy had responded to her call and were waiting for her. Godwin was all agog to

229

know what this was about.

"I'm going to show you how I think Ryan McMurphy was murdered," she said, leading them into the rear half of the shop, where the many painted needlepoint canvases lived, along with the wools and silks and flosses necessary to complete them.

"Let this bucket be Shelly's sewing room," said Betsy. It was a tall white plastic bucket that had once held forty pounds of kitty litter.

"Kind of a small workspace," noted Leona.

"Nice high ceilings, however," said Godwin.

Mike snorted softly.

Betsy took a small candle set into a frosted glass globe, open at the top, and put it into the bucket. She said, "Shelly likes a really well-lit work space, so when the lights are on, it's blinding bright in there. Ryan was afraid of the dark, but couldn't sleep in the bright light. So he would put a candle in a big pottery bowl — the bowl was because he was also afraid of fire — and light it. He'd leave it lit and it would be burned out by morning." She struck a match and lit the candle.

Then, using a plastic spoon, she scooped up a few pellets of dry ice from the plastic

230

bag, whose top she had cut open. Two tumbled off the spoon, and without thinking she grabbed for them, caught one, and yelled in pain. She shook it out of her hand onto the floor.

"It *burned* me!" she exclaimed, looking at the dark red shape forming on the palm of her left hand.

Mike took her hand. "That's a bad burn," he said frowning at it. "What'd you grab it for?"

"It was just instinct," she said, squeezing her left wrist hard. "But how do I make it stop hurting? If it was a regular burn, I'd put ice on it."

Leona said, "Let me see." She took Betsy's hand from Mike and held it gently. She closed her eyes and suddenly Betsy felt the pain go away.

"What — How did you do that?" Betsy asked.

"It's a talent I got from my grandmother. It's called 'drawing fire.' I wasn't sure it would work on that, since it's not hot, but I guess it does."

Mike made a grimace of disbelief, but Godwin was awestruck. "That is the most *fantastic* thing I have ever *seen!* It's, it's like a *miracle!*" He grinned. "Or is it magic?"

"No, it's not magic, and it's not a miracle,

231

either. It's just a natural talent some people have," said Leona, her tone patient. "Like water witching, which my father could do. Now, my dear," she continued to Betsy, "go on with this interesting experiment."

Working more carefully, Betsy scattered four two-inch-long pellets of dry ice into the bucket.

"Now what?" asked Mike.

"Now we wait."

"Aren't you going to pour in a little water?" asked Godwin. "That's how you get the vapor."

"No, the water just makes the vapor visible. It's there."

It took about five minutes. The pellets dwindled just a little but the air around them didn't look any different.

"Watch," said Betsy at last, noticing the candle starting to fade, and the four heads came together over the top of the bucket.

Very quietly, and with no signs of a struggle, the candle's flame grew smaller and weaker. It finally went out, sending a thin streamer of smoke upward.

"So?" said Mike.

"It was the carbon dioxide that smothered the flame," said Betsy. "Dry ice goes directly from solid to gas, no liquid in between. And it replaces the air in the room, killing anything that demands oxygen, such as a candle. Or a human being. That's why there was half a candle left beside Ryan's body."

"I nearly died when I got too close to the dry ice fog at Rafael's party," said Godwin.

"But you didn't die — because you were found and moved into fresh air in time," said Betsy. She and Godwin explained to Mike the incident at the party. She concluded, "There was no one to do that for Ryan."

"But he would have seen the fog!" objected Mike. "I've been around dry ice fog lots of times. Even without water, there's a kind of fog."

Betsy pointed to the bucket. "You just saw it at work here. When the air is dry, there is little or no fog. And remember, Ryan was in no condition to notice a faint fog in the air if there was one," she said.

"Light that candle again," ordered Mike. "I want to see if that experiment works twice in a row."

But they couldn't light the candle again. Carbon dioxide is heavier than air, and it filled the bottom quarter of the bucket. Every time Betsy lowered a lit match beyond a certain point, it went out. She could lift the candle out and light it, but lowering it into the bucket was like lowering it into water: it went out instantly.

"Okay, how do you get rid of it?" asked Mike. "The gas, I mean."

"It dissipates all by itself. That's why Shelly could walk in the next day with no harm. Do you want to stay and wait to see how long it takes? In the sewing room it had the rest of the night and half the next day."

"I don't want to stand here for the rest of the day," said Mike. He upended the bucket, "pouring out" the carbon dioxide. It took several tries and some forceful swirling of the bucket before the bottom was clear enough of the gas to support a candle flame. "How much dry ice does it take to kill a person anyhow?" he wondered.

"That's not an experiment I'm willing to try," said Betsy. "But it displaces the air when it first evaporates. They warned me at Metro Ice to use this only in a ventilated room."

"Okay, but how did it get in there? The door was locked, remember? Shelly had to unlock it to get to McMurphy."

Betsy said, "I'm thinking there were two ways. First, it could have been put in there before he got home. The door was not locked when he wasn't there. The question is, how far in advance could the killer put it in there? Ryan was undressed and in bed when he was found, so the gas couldn't have been very concentrated when he got home, or he would have passed out on the floor. And how would the killer know when he was coming home?"

"He couldn't," Mike said. "When McMurphy was out on the town, he'd come home at all different times. He stayed either until he got thrown out, or the tavern closed. There was no way to tell in advance when he was coming home to that basement room."

"Well, that brings us to the second possibility. It might have been someone with a key, someone who waited until he was in there and asleep — or passed out — before entering to put the dry ice in a bucket. And they'd have had to use a bucket, I suppose, because won't this substance damage a carpet or wood floor?" She turned around to look for the dropped pellets and used the plastic spoon to pick them up and drop them into the bucket. To her surprise, there was no trace of their presence on her Berber carpet. She stooped and ran her fingers over places they had been, looking for stiffness, bleaching, or other damage, and found nothing but two cool, faintly damp spots. "Humph, I guess not."

Mike said, "The candle tells us something. It was burnt just about halfway down when it went out."

Betsy said, "I lit one last night — the same kind of candle — and found out it burns at a rate of about an inch an hour. And they're five inches tall, so halfway is two and a half hours. It went out two and a half hours after it was lit."

Malloy said, "The medical examiner says that Ryan McMurphy died around three in the morning. And I found someone who says he brought Ryan home around midnight, so figure he took half an hour to get ready for bed and light his candle and that's about right."

"But that would mean someone came in right after he got into bed, which sounds unlikely. I would think the murderer would wait until he was sure Ryan was sound asleep."

"Oh, those time of death things aren't an exact science," said Mike. "I'd say there's probably half an hour leeway on either side of that estimate. And I'd also guess, from the description of how drunk McMurphy was that night, that he was unconscious the second his head hit the pillow."

"Is three hours enough time for dry ice to fill that room?" asked Godwin.

"It didn't have to fill it to the top," said Betsy, "just the bottom third should have done it."

Mike said, "I'll check it out, how long it would take." He gave a sharp glance at Betsy. "But you know what this means. Unless you're going to try to prove them innocent."

"Not Shelly," said Betsy positively. "I've known her since my first day in Excelsior, and she works for me part-time. Under no circumstances would I believe that Shelly did this."

Mike nodded at her. Unspoken between them lay Harvey's name.

Betsy had a thought. She said, "Mike, check to see if anyone heard the dog barking. Maybe Shelly and Harv were out, so the killer sneaked in. But Shelly says the dog barks."

"All right." Mike made a note.

Betsy turned to Godwin and Leona. "May I ask you not to repeat any of this conversation to anyone? Not about the dry ice as a murder weapon and especially not about who Mike suspects. Nothing is proven yet."

"I know only too well the power of unproven accusations in Excelsior," said Leona with emphasis.

After Mike and Leona left, Betsy put the

extinguished candle, still in its globe, in a desk drawer. She put the plastic bag of dry ice into the bucket and took it out to the Dumpster in the parking lot behind the shop.

"Goddy," she said on returning, "don't tell anyone about Leona taking the pain out of my hand."

"Why not?" he demanded. "It was a fabulous thing she did."

"Because one of the reasons she hasn't been hounded out of town is that a majority of the residents don't believe in witchcraft. Their disbelief is keeping her safe. You start offering them evidence to the contrary, all the dry ice in the county won't help."

FIFTEEN

A few customers later — Godwin biting his tongue with obvious effort to keep from telling about the marvel of Leona "drawing fire" — Billie came in.

"I'm in a knitting mood," she announced. "Wool me!"

Godwin helped her select two skeins of cherry red wool, a pattern for a spiral pattern scarf, and a new set of number eight bamboo knitting needles.

Checking out at the desk, she said to Betsy, "How's the investigation coming?"

"It's just about at a halt right now," said Betsy, putting Billie's purchases into a Crewel World plastic drawstring bag. "I *think* I know how it was done, but I can't figure out who might have done it."

"But you know how?" Billie was staring at her. "You're serious! You mean it wasn't black magic?"

"No, of course not."

"That sounds . . . strange. I've heard that Ryan locked the door to the sewing room when he was in there. That seems to mean it was Shelly or Harv. But that doesn't sound like them at all. I mean, if they wanted Ryan out, all they had to do was tell him to leave."

"I know. That's what makes it so depressing."

"So really you have no suspects at all," said Billie, sounding disappointed.

"Oh, no, I have suspects. It's just that they have alibis. You, for example."

"Me?"

Betsy smiled. "Yes, you. Someone told me you hated Ryan. Is that true?"

"I didn't hate him. Okay, I was mad at him for a long time. But hate? No. It's a wearisome thing, and a waste of time." She smiled. "Almost as tiresome a thing as the Halloween festival. Aren't you tired of all the planning for it?"

"Oh, yes. And I'm going to get tired of Christmas long before it arrives. It's one of the sad parts of being in commerce. But why were you mad at him for a long time?"

"Because he kept my daughter Cara out of the Naval Academy."

It was Betsy's turn to look surprised. "How did he manage to do that?"

"Well, he and Cara are cousins, you know."

"No, I didn't know that."

Billie nodded. "His mother and my husband are brother and sister. Cara decided halfway through high school that she wanted to follow another cousin into the Naval Academy — Sunny is doing work she loves, and the education she got was simply superb. But Cara had slacked off during her sophomore year, and although she was working very hard to bring her grades up, things looked marginal for her. Sunny wrote a letter to our Congressman in Washington recommending her, and she helped Cara write her own letter. And, of course, her father and I also wrote letters, and got two of her teachers to write as well. And we got some very encouraging replies from Congressman Karlson.

"Then Sunny and Ryan had a falling out — Ryan was always quarreling with someone or other — and he decided that the way to get back at Sunny was to bollix her attempts to help Cara get into the Academy. So when Representative Karlson sent some staff member around to see what sort of person Cara was, he made sure to spread the word about Cara's shooting a deer out of season, making her sound like a poacher."

Betsy could only blink at this. "She poached a deer?"

"Of course not! It was just a stupid mistake. There were these deer invading our vegetable garden, eating simply everything. We'd put up a fence but it wasn't high enough. Cara wanted to enter some of her tomatoes and pumpkins in the County Fair, and what the deer didn't eat, they trampled. So she sat up one night with her dad's thirty-ought-six rifle, meaning just to fire over their heads and scare them, and one deer jumped the fence just as she fired and she brought it down. She didn't tell us until the next morning, by which time she had it hanging in the garage, and her boyfriend helping her turn it into roasts and steaks. She was surprised we didn't think it was just a funny accident and begged us not to report it, so we didn't, but she'd already told some other friends. It wasn't all that serious, though I didn't agree it was a joke." Billie smiled. "One thing it did do, the other deer left the garden alone for the rest of the growing season.

"But Ryan told a colorized version to people, and he said she cheated on her final exam in calculus, and by the time his stories got back to Congressman Karlson's representative, it was all exaggerated, like she

242

cheated on all her exams and that she shot that deer on purpose. And so Cara didn't get the appointment."

"Oh, that's too bad."

"Yes, it was, and I was very angry with Ryan for a long while. But I told Cara to go to my alma mater and join ROTC" — Billie pronounced it *Rot-Cee* — "and she tried that, but there is an anti-ROTC culture at that university and she decided she didn't like college after all. Now she's finishing up a veterinary assistant course at Minneapolis Technical College and she's doing well."

"I suppose she was angry at Ryan?"

"Oh, lord yes."

"Billie, is it possible that *Cara* is responsible for Ryan's death?"

Billie went white. *"Of course not!"*

"Do you know where she was the night Ryan died?"

"How dare you even *think* — wait a minute!" Billie brightened, her expression turning in an instant from that of a mother bear protecting her cub almost to glee. "She was in Chicago at a science fiction convention. Didn't get home till Tuesday noon. Whew! For a minute there, you really scared me."

"Let me scare you again: Where were *you?*"

But Billie wasn't worried. "Oh, I was home. I get nervous when Cara's traveling, I wake up three times a night, and my getting up wakes Sam — he's *such* a light sleeper. 'What the hell time is it now?' he'll ask. So he can tell you I was home in bed, out of bed, back in bed with him all night every night starting the Thursday before. Sunday night we went to bed around ten-thirty, after the news."

Betsy wasn't sure Sam wouldn't lie for his wife, but she didn't say so.

Billie said, "Are you all set for the parade? Do you know the marching order yet?"

Betsy picked up a notebook and turned to a page full of cross-outs, interlineations, notes, lines and arrows, and listings. "I'm going to make a clean copy of this before the parade, of course. We've got three bands now. That should be enough, don't you think?"

"Yes, probably. Do you have enough candy clowns?"

"I've got a half dozen. One of the clowns has a pretty scary costume. Is that all right?"

"Depends on how scary. They're going to be marching along the edges of the parade and coming close to the children to toss them the candy. If it'll scare a three-year-old, you'd better lighten it up."

Betsy made yet another note on the page. "Okay."

"Anything else?"

"Joey Mitchell wants to drive the fire engine. I told him to contact LuLu McMurphy, since the truck is hers now."

"He did that, and she said she didn't care who drove it, so I told him he could."

"Good," said Betsy, making yet another note.

"Anything else?"

"No, everything else seems to be in order."

And it was — the parade part, anyhow. The investigation? Not so much.

Near closing time, the door to Crewel World opened and Harvey came in, his face white and set in a grim expression. "Ms. Devonshire, I want to talk to you," he said in a low but angry voice. He took her by the arm and marched her through the back of the shop, where there were no customers, into the tiny back room, closing the door behind them.

"Where the *hell* do you get off telling Mike Malloy you think I murdered Ryan McMurphy?" he demanded, his voice even angrier than before.

"I did not tell Sergeant Malloy that I thought you were a murderer," Betsy replied in as level a voice as she could manage. "But someone brought a poisonous substance into Shelly's sewing room the night Ryan died, probably after he went in there and locked the door. There were only two keys to that door, and Ryan had one of them. The conclusion was not hard to draw. I didn't have to point anything out to Mike Malloy."

"But I didn't have a *motive!*"

"Didn't you? Mr. Fogelman, are you a married man?"

He sucked air through his teeth. *"Who told you that?"*

"No one. But when I suggested blackmail to you in Chanhassen the day before yesterday, you ran off like a scalded fox. And Shelly is starting to wonder if you'll ever ask her to marry you. The Hennepin County records of marriages and divorces indicate that you married one Melissa Jean Brooks nearly thirty years ago, but not that you divorced her. Nor is there a record of her death. The conclusion is obvious. Less obvious is why you insisted that Ryan be permitted to remain in Shelly's house when he became a drunken, obnoxious menace."

He stared at her, and suddenly his anger drained away. "I didn't kill him," he said.

"Well, I don't think Shelly did," she said.

246

"Shelly? Of course not!" He sounded shocked that Betsy could even suggest such a thing.

"Then who else had a key?" she asked.

Just then, the door to the back room opened and Godwin stood there with a heavy stitching frame in one hand. "Is everything all right in here?" he asked in his deepest voice, hefting the frame.

"Yes, we're fine," said Betsy.

"I have to go," said Harvey, and he brushed roughly past Godwin on his way out.

The shop was closed, and Betsy was taking out the trash. She lifted the heavy, creaky, squealing lid of the Dumpster and got a noseful of something acidic and tingling.

"Whuff!" she said, backing away. Then she went for a more careful look and, to her amazement, the plastic bag of dry ice was still mostly full. Water vapor was curling up and out of the bucket. The inside of the Dumpster was damp — not from the rain but condensation — and very chilly, colder than the outside air.

The effect on her nose made her think of the times she'd been too eager to get a swallow of Coke after opening a can. It wasn't cola up the nose; it was freshly released carbon dioxide. How interesting to learn that!

And also how interesting about the condensation. That was very likely the explanation for Shelly's rusty needles.

But most interesting of all was the fact that the dry ice was still there. It had been sitting in the Dumpster for hours. She stood there a minute or two, thinking. If it always took a long time to evaporate, that meant the dry ice could have been put into Shelly's sewing room far earlier than she had originally thought. Hours earlier. Shelly had been using the room when Ryan was out; it was locked only when he was in there. She needed to find out if Shelly had been in the room on Sunday.

She hustled back into the shop and called Shelly on her cell. But when Shelly answered, her voice sounded strange. Betsy could tell she was in tears.

"Shelly, what's the matter?"

"It's Harv. Betsy, he's *married.* He just told me."

"Oh, Shelly, I'm so sorry to hear that."

"He's been trying to find her. She moved out of town years ago, and he doesn't know where she is. He didn't used to care; he didn't want to get married again. But now he does, and he needs to find her to file for

248

divorce. I *knew* something was wrong, but I never figured it was *this!* He just came in a little while ago and he was all upset. He was almost crying, and it took me a while to get it out of him, but now I'm all upset, too! Oh, Betsy, I'm so *unhappy!* What are we going to *do?*"

Betsy shoved her fingers into her hair. "I don't know what to tell you. What else did he say? Has this got anything to do with Ryan?"

"What could it have to do with Ryan?"

"Well, I wonder if Ryan knew and that's how he persuaded Harv to get you to let him move into your sewing room."

There was a shocked silence. Betsy could tell that Shelly was considering the possibility.

"Shelly, where were you and Harv that Sunday evening?"

"Oh, *Betsy!* How *dare* you think —"

"Shelly, please! I'm trying to help you, don't you understand that?"

Silence fell again. Then, in a very subdued voice, Shelly said, "We were out. We went to see my Aunt Sally. I don't think you've ever met her — she's a retired schoolteacher and she lives in White Bear Lake. We had dinner at her place and then sat and talked until probably close to ten o'clock. Then we came home and went right to bed."

"Both of you?"

"Both of us."

"What time did you leave for White Bear?"

"Around five-thirty."

White Bear Lake was to the north and east of Saint Paul, a good forty-five minutes from Excelsior.

"Who knew you were going over there for a visit?"

"Oh, gosh, lots of people. Going to see Aunt Sally is a real treat, and both of us talked about it."

Betsy thanked her, told her not to worry, and hung up.

So the two of them were out of the house until near eleven o'clock Sunday night. That brought them home a little more than an hour before Ryan.

Was that enough time for Shelly to go to bed and fall so deeply asleep that Harvey could get up without waking her to go put dry ice into the sewing room?

Could he have put it in there before they left?

Which brought another thought: Where did he keep it? Not the freezer, Shelly might see it. So possibly an ice chest down in the basement or on the back porch, because who opens an ice chest in October? But where — and when — did he get it? It used to be, you could get dry ice at any store that sold regular ice, especially if it also sold live bait — fishermen used dry ice to keep their fish fresh on the sometimes long journey home. But when Betsy went looking for dry ice on the Internet, she couldn't find a regular business that sold it, only wholesalers. And they weren't open on Sundays.

All right, things were looking a little better for Harvey Fogelman. So suppose someone else put it in there. When? Certainly not while Shelly and Harvey were there and still up. ("Excuse me, just making a delivery of dry ice, pay no attention to me.")

Betsy knew that Shelly, like many residents of Excelsior, didn't lock her outside doors; therefore, anyone wanting to get into the house while they were gone didn't need a key. So long as not enough dry ice had evaporated to cause the nose-tingling effect or to make the candle impossible to light, Ryan might not have noticed the room was filling with it when he got home. Especially if he was drunk — and the medical examiner had said he was.

She went back inside to search the Internet, and found a web site maintained by a scientist named Dr. Robert Sherman who was advising businesses about the uses of dry ice. Sandblasting was one suggestion. She shot him an e-mail asking how long it would take dry ice vapor to fill the bottom third of a twelve-by-ten room.

To her amazement, Dr. Sherman was online and he replied immediately. "I hope you are aware of the dangers of doing such a thing," he wrote.

"Yes, very," replied Betsy. "Someone here in town was killed because of carbon dioxide, and I'm investigating the case."

"All right. To answer your question: About four hours, if the room is above sixty-five degrees, the dry ice is in pellets, spread out a little and not piled in a heap," wrote Dr. Sherman. "Six hours if it's a block."

Up to six hours. That meant someone could have gone in while Ryan, Shelly, and Harvey were all three out and left enough dry ice to stealthily replace the breathable air in the room.

It also meant that none of Betsy's suspects had an alibi anymore.

Sixteen

"Bing-bong!" announced the door. Betsy often wished it could announce more than merely the entrance of a potential customer. Then perhaps she would not walk out of the bathroom, where she'd been evicting a spider, into the gaze of a strange man while her nose was ornamented with a smear of dust and a fragment of spider web hung from her left earring.

Because the doorbell was unable to warn her to glance in the mirror before coming out, she spent the entire conversation wondering what he thought was so funny every time he looked at her.

"Are you Ms. Devonshire?" he asked, pronouncing it correctly, Devon-Sheer. He was about her age, mid-fifties, not-quite-skinny but with broad shoulders. His hair was black and curly, going to gray on the sides.

"Yes?"

"I'm Connor Sullivan, and I understand you have an apartment to rent."

"I have two, actually, or I will in another month. The one that's vacant now is the smaller of the two. Would you like to see it?"

"Yes, very much, thank you."

Betsy looked around to tell Godwin where she was going, but he had already anticipated her next move. "You go ahead, we've got things under control down here," he said, giving her an amused look. She frowned at him, and he brushed his nose, as if embarrassed. She did, too, and he nodded.

Satisfied, she turned away and so missed his earlobe-pulling gesture.

Mr. Sullivan's face was deeply lined, his eyes dark and hooded. His hands had the thickened, callused look that comes only from hard physical work. He wore jeans and walking shoes, and a beautiful Aran sweater on which beads of water stood up like opals. Clearly it had started to rain again.

She led him upstairs and unlocked the door to Doris's old apartment. It still smelled faintly of fresh paint. Because it was small, Betsy had selected light colors for its decor. The living room was a very pale yellow, barely more than a rich cream, walls and ceiling alike. The drapes were the color called old gold, the carpet sky blue. The blue carpet continued into the bedroom, but here the walls were a pale blue.

"As you can see, the apartment is unfurnished. For an increase in rent, I can furnish it."

"No, I have furniture," he said. He was looking around with a critical but approving eye. He thumped a wall with a knuckle, testing its thickness. "How old is this building?" he asked.

"Built in 1910," she said.

"Very good," he said. "I like old places."

The bathroom was a model of efficiency, and Betsy had spent money on bronze and brown natural tile, even to a raised frieze of fish about halfway up the tub-shower enclosure.

Mr. Sullivan nodded his approval.

The kitchen had Corian counters in dark green, and there was a light green and blue glass tile backsplash along the wall, under the pale wood cabinets and over the stainless steel sink. The refrigerator and stove were new, the floor an imitation stone tile. "Real tile is hard on your feet," Sullivan noted approvingly as he cast a cook's eye on the arrangements. Lots of lighting and a big opening into the living room helped to disguise the fact that there were no windows in the kitchen.

"Very snug," was his final remark on the place.

"Would you like to see the other apartment?" Betsy asked. "It will be available in about three weeks. It comes furnished."

"No, no, I think I like this very well. Do you rent from month to month, or would you prefer that a tenant sign a lease?"

"A one-year lease would be good," she said.

They went back downstairs and Betsy gave him a copy of the lease to look over.

"When would you want to move in?" she asked impulsively. With that question, she cut out the several people ahead of him in line.

"Would November first be all right?" he asked.

"That would be fine." She walked him to the door, and as he turned to say good-bye, he said, "I see you've got a broken door over here." His light tone took the sting out of the implied criticism of her shop.

"Yes, I keep meaning to call a handyman about it. I'll get on that today."

"Would you like me to fix it for you?"

"What, are you a cabinetmaker?"

"In an amateur way, yes." Again he spoke

lightly, but somehow Betsy had no doubt he could do it.

Still, "Let me get back to you," she said.

After he left, Godwin came up to the table, where Betsy was returning to her task of putting together little kits of Christmas ornaments in clear plastic bags. These would be kept in a basket by the checkout desk for impulse buyers.

"He likes you," he said with a hint of a leer.

"Who likes me?" she asked absentmindedly, sliding a tiny sprig of plastic holly onto the ribbon that was holding the plastic bag shut.

"That man who just rented Doris's apartment. He really likes you."

She looked up at him. "Just because you've found a new love, you think you see it everywhere! Honestly, Goddy! And anyway, he hasn't rented it yet. He just took a copy of the lease to look at." She shook her head at him, and he pulled a handkerchief from his pocket, leaned toward her, and captured the little length of spider web from her left ear. He showed it to her before putting the handkerchief away.

"Oh, for cripe's sake!" she groaned, and he laughed.

■ ■ ■ ■

Three hours later, Betsy was alone in the shop when Shelly came in with a flat Tupperware cake pan. Inside it, wrapped in many layers of tissue paper, was a small, counted-cross-stitch piece of fabric.

Done in shades of purple, lavender, and silver-gray, with touches of silver and black metallics, it was a witch's hat in a sturdy frame of cross-stitch counterchanged in light and dark lavender, the space between the hat and frame filled with a net of delicate blackwork lightly strewn with tiny leaves. The stitching was done in silk, which gave it a subtle shine, as if it were seen in a half-light — very appropriate for the theme.

"Well, this is *nice,* very balanced and attractive!" Betsy said. "May I ask you where you got the blackwork pattern?" Because it looked familiar.

"It's mine. I mean, there are only so many variables you can do in blackwork; the vine-and-leaf, for example, is a common motif. But the pattern layout is my very own."

"I like the way it fills the space without overwhelming it. Kreinik should be pleased."

"Thank you, I hope so. See that dark

purple there? That's going to be their newest color in silk. If they like this pattern, they'll use it to introduce the color."

"Wow, that means it will get worldwide distribution! How nice for you!"

Shelly simpered just a little, then said, "It needs to be finished quickly — can you or even Heidi send it directly to Kreinik? I can tell them it's coming."

"I'll call Heidi today." Heidi Watgren was a finisher, a person who took a piece of completed needlework to wash it, stretch and dry it, mat and frame it. It was an expensive service, but a piece that was to become a family heirloom or a published design deserved special treatment.

Shelly said, "It's not to be matted and framed, okay?"

"Then why don't you wash and stretch it yourself?"

"Oh, I'm too nervous. What if the colors run, or I stretch it all out of shape? I want an expert's hands on it at this late stage. This is too important to risk a finishing mistake."

"I understand completely. Do you want it sent in the Tupperware?"

"Oh, gosh, no! I want a proper mailing box for it. You can use the tissue paper, however. Here's the pattern, and here's the

259

address." Shelly handed over a sheet of typing paper and a three-by-five card on which was very carefully printed the address of Kreinik Manufacturing in West Virginia.

"All right, fine. I'll let you know the day it goes into the mail."

Betsy hesitated to ask her next question, but she felt she had to know. "Shelly, may I ask you what you're going to do about Harvey?"

"I've told him he has to move out until the mess with his first marriage is fixed." She added unhappily, "However long it takes."

"You could suggest that he hire a licensed private investigator to find his wife."

Shelly frowned at her. "Would that be a good idea?"

"They do it all the time. There even used to be a radio show about it. Godwin told me about Mr. Keen, tracer of lost persons."

If Shelly was happy about getting her project finished, she was ecstatic about the PI notion. "I'll tell him!" she declared, and hurried out of the shop.

"Rafael, I think we may have to do something about her! Or him! Or him and her!" Godwin sounded anxious.

"Why should we have to do something,

Gorrión? They are adults — more adult than either of us, for that matter. She is what, in her later fifties?"

"That's not the *point*. The point is, she is very bad at picking men. She lets the right one get away and she marries the wrong one!"

"And yet you brought me around for her to judge if I was right for you."

"About other people, she's amazing. It's about herself that she's hopeless."

"Well, what do you propose that we do?"

"That's what I'm hoping you can think of."

Rafael looked fondly at Godwin. "You are such an idiot, you know that? How am I to know such a thing?"

"Maybe if we put our heads together, we can think of something."

"Better that we try to persuade her to stop meddling in police business. Do you know how dangerous that can be? She could find herself the subject of an investigation! Or worse, the victim of a murderer!"

"No, she's very careful, truly she is." But Godwin felt uneasy saying that. *After all, Patricia Fairland could have killed her,* he thought. He had often wondered himself why his boss felt drawn to sleuthing. It was exciting and interesting, but like Rafael said, it could be dangerous.

"Suppose I were to be a criminal, would she investigate me? And how would you feel about that?"

"Are you a dangerous criminal?"

"I'm sure I have broken many laws. It is impossible to live long in any country without breaking a few laws."

"What laws have you broken?"

"Oh, I have murdered quite a few people. Not any important ones, however."

Godwin stared at him, then the two started laughing.

The next day Betsy went out for lunch, walking over to The Barleywine. She saw Leona behind the bar talking with a patron and approached. The patron was saying, "I just put my first IPA in the primary and I'm hoping you can give me some direction on dry hopping the secondary. I formulated my own recipe, and my OG was one point oh eight oh, and the IBUs between a hundred and one oh five. I was going to dry hop in the secondary an ounce whole leaf cascade the first week, a one-ounce pellet Centennial the second week. I figured I'd brew the first twelve days at sixty-eight degrees, the last two days much lower to settle, then bottle — but that was based on a recipe with lower OG and IBUs. Is two weeks in a secondary good enough for the higher gravity and IBUs?"

Betsy hesitated. Technical talk could be lengthy, and this fellow had a lengthy question.

But Leona just said, "It all depends on what you want the aroma, taste, mouth feel, and appearance to be like. I'd do twelve days in the secondary with the first dry hop, the last four days at forty-two degrees to clear the beer, then bottle." Then she looked up and saw Betsy, and waved her over.

As Betsy approached, the patron said, "Thanks, Leona," and retired to a booth with his mug of beer.

Leona asked Betsy, "What can I do for you?"

"I'd like a burger, medium rare, with lettuce and tomato, and potato chips, and a cup of tea, please." She glanced over her shoulder at the patron. "You know, I had no idea how complicated beer making is."

"It's as simple or complicated as you care to make it. The more you look for a reliable product, the more careful you are about your recipe. But you can't get so careful that you never try anything new."

"And speaking of that, what's new with you?"

"I've been experimenting with pumpkin beer, and I think we've got a good one right now. But what I'm doing now is making pumpkin pie with the leavings. Care for a slice?"

Betsy smiled. "Yes, if you'll change my order to a chef salad. But does the pie smell of beer?"

"Not so's you'd notice."

"What made you think to try it anyhow? Is it a lambic beer like the cherry and peach?"

"No, it's an early American idea. In the Colonies, barley was expensive and hard to come by, so people made beer out of pumpkins. But this is my own version of the recipe, because it's got brown sugar and nutmeg in it — and sugar and spices were even harder to come by than barley in the white man's early days on this continent. One of the bonuses of pumpkin beer is that you can get pumpkin pie from what's left behind after straining the mash. I found the recipe in a magazine for amateur brewers, a guy named Mark Pasquinelli came up with it — including the pumpkin pie idea."

"Okay, I'd love a slice of pie — but I hope you're right about it not tasting of beer. I have to be careful of my breath when I'm in the shop. Do you have milk on your menu?

I think nothing tastes as good with pumpkin pie as milk."

"Certainly. Chef salad, pumpkin pie, milk. I'll get your order in right now."

Leona disappeared into the kitchen area of the brew-pub.

Betsy looked around. Besides the patron with the brewing question, there was only one other customer. Normally, the place would be crowded with people eating lunch. The way he was dressed made it clear that the one customer was a businessman, and he was finishing up a sandwich and a cup of coffee.

By the time Leona came back, he was standing at the cash register at the far end of the bar, with his credit card in hand. He did not speak to Leona beyond the word or two necessary to complete his transaction, and he went out into the noontime's vague sunlight without a word of good-bye.

Betsy looked at Leona, feeling a stab of compassion.

Leona nodded. "We really need to clear this up, Betsy," she said.

"I agree. And I'm trying. I came over here to talk to Billie."

"She's got the day off, and she's got a list a mile long of things she needs to get done before the Halloween thing kicks off on

Saturday."

"May I ask you some questions, then?"

"Certainly."

"When you told me you were here at The Barleywine on Sunday, did you mean you were back in the brewery area or out front here?"

"Out front. And let me tell you, the only thing harder on the feet than that tile floor in the brewery is the slate floor we put in here. If we ever get far enough into the black, I'm going to replace it."

Betsy looked down at the irregular slabs that had likely cost a pretty penny to buy, install, and seal. The floor looked beautiful, but doubtless Leona was right — it looked like it would be hard on the feet.

"Maybe just replace it behind the bar," Betsy suggested.

Leona said, "Now that's probably a good idea." She nodded to herself, storing the suggestion away, then said, "Why are you asking about an earlier alibi? Has the medical examiner changed his estimate of time of death?"

"No, but that method I think was used could have been set up as many as six hours before Ryan died."

" 'As many as'? Does that mean there's a big spread?"

"Yes," said Betsy.

"Well, doesn't *that* just make your task a whole lot easier!" Leona's tone was sympathetic.

Just then, the door to the kitchen opened and a young woman Betsy recognized as a part-timer in her shop came into the pub. She was holding a tray with Betsy's salad, pie, and milk. She smiled at Betsy. "Well, hello!" she said. "Good to see not everyone's staying away!"

"No, of course they aren't," said Betsy loyally. "And the rest will be back soon, you'll see."

"Glad to hear it," said the woman, and she went back into the kitchen.

"You want to ask me something else?" prompted Leona.

"How well do you know Joey Mitchell?" Betsy dug into her salad.

"I've known him since he was a kid. His parents used to bring him into the Waterfront Café about twice a month — his dad was a volunteer fireman, you know."

"Yes, I've heard that a lot of his family members were firefighters."

"It does run in families. His great-grandfather was also a fireman in Minneapolis, during World War Two."

Betsy said, "So he must've been really

upset when he had to stop being a fireman because of his arm."

"He hated Ryan for a long time. I think if he could have called him out, gotten into a fistfight with him, it would have done both of them a world of good — it ate at Ryan, too, you know."

"I hadn't thought of it from that angle. Yet Ryan wouldn't quit drinking."

"Couldn't quit. Not for good anyway. I don't think anyone fully understands the dynamics of alcoholism. The triggers that set off binges in people are as individual as they are, probably."

"What started him in again that last Thursday he was in here?"

"Goddess knows. I certainly don't. Did anyone criticize his work on the fire engine?"

"On the contrary, everyone was very pleased and said so. Especially Billie."

"Ah, yes, Billie and Ryan, there's an interesting story."

"Yes, she told me. Do you know where she was on Sunday?"

"If you mean, was I with her the whole time, no."

"Did you see her at all?"

"Oh, yes," said Leona, "she came in to see if the repairman had come to fix the refrigerator in the kitchen — he had, and about time! — and she ate lunch here."

"How about later?"

"She had the mayor to supper here, and then had coffee with two members of our Chamber of Commerce. I really don't think she should have taken on the job of running our Halloween event; it's been driving her crazy. Between that, running her house, and working here, she doesn't have time for a nervous breakdown. Like the old joke goes, as soon as the rush is over, she'll have one. She's worked for it, she's earned it, and no one is going to keep her from it."

Betsy chuckled. Old folks like old jokes best. She said, "This salad is great."

"Just like you remember it, right? Down to the hard-boiled egg wedges."

"You bet." Betsy was feeling older by the second.

"So how is the parade planning coming along?"

"My part in it? Just fine. I figure so long as I don't put the three bands right behind one another, it'll work out great. How come Billie didn't persuade you to take a role?"

"Because All Hallows is a religious holiday for me."

"You really are serious about your religion, aren't you?"

"Aren't you about yours?"

"Yes, I suppose I am. And I'm a little ashamed to say you probably know a whole lot more about Christianity than I do about Wicca."

"I could loan you a nice, thick book."

"Which would sit unread on my coffee table until I felt safe returning it — I'm a busy person, too, Leona."

Leona laughed.

"May I ask a possibly insulting question about Wicca?"

"Certainly."

"Surely you don't really believe in things like the Wendigo, or tree sprites. So how can you think there are gods of the storm and sea?"

"Have you ever read Rudyard Kipling's *Just So Stories*?" asked Leona.

"Of course," said Betsy, puzzled by this sudden shift of topic.

"Remember 'The Elephant's Child'?"

Betsy smiled. "Yes, about how the elephant got his long trunk."

"How did that happen?"

Still smiling, Betsy replied, "The insatiably curious baby elephant poked his little nose into the great gray-green greasy Limpopo River, all set about with fever trees; and a crocodile grabbed hold and stretched it out."

"Do you believe that story? Do you think it's really how the elephant got his trunk?"

"No, of course not!"

"Does that mean there are no such things as elephants?"

"Oh," said Betsy.

The pumpkin pie was delicious.

SEVENTEEN

The rest of the day didn't help narrow down the list of suspects much. On the phone, LuLu McMurphy confessed that both her daughters went to a playdate at a neighbor's house for an hour after supper at five, so she had no alibi for the early evening of the day Ryan was murdered.

"How well do you know Shelly Donohue?" Betsy asked as talk drifted to other subjects.

"Oh, gosh, I've known Shelly since grade school," LuLu replied, "and Harv for about three years. They seem to be good for each other. At first I didn't think they'd be a match, since she comes from a white-collar family and I was sure he was a blue-collar type. All that outdoor stuff, you know. I thought it was mostly lawn mowing and tree trimming. It was Ryan who made me understand there was a creative mind shining brightly among all the foliage — those two have been friends for years. He really is brilliant, you know. Harv, I mean. He can look at a dreary piece of land and make a plan for a beautiful garden."

"How did he come to let Ryan stay with them? Didn't Shelly throw a fit? I know I would've."

"She did. Harv was for letting him use the spare bedroom, but Shelly said it had too much of her stuff in it, and Ryan was a snoop as well as a gossip. Harv was supposed to help her turn it into a proper guest room, but that's one of those projects that just wasn't getting done, you know?"

Betsy, thinking of the broken door in the Crewel World counter, nodded.

"Since it was only supposed to be for a couple of days, Harv borrowed a futon from someone he works with and set it up on the floor of the sewing room. But it went on and on. Shelly was already at the end of her rope after nine days when Ryan called to say he'd been arrested for drunk driving and causing an accident. She told Harv in no uncertain terms that that was it, Ryan was out. But he talked her around somehow. Harv came and begged me to take Ryan back. I said my terms were he enters a resident treatment center and joins AA afterward. But Ryan was still convinced he could beat this on his own."

"Do you think it's possible that Harv or Shelly could be responsible for Ryan's death?"

She smiled. "Over him sleeping in Shelly's sewing room? No. Harv is not the type to kill anyone, unless maybe he caught him harming Shelly. He really, really loves her — I'm surprised they aren't married. Of course, he had a disastrous first marriage; Ryan said something about it to me."

"What did he say?"

"He said he tried to tease Harv about it and Harv told him if he brought her up again he'd murder him." She made a choking sound and hastened to add, "No, no, that's a joke! It was just a joke! Ryan liked to say things to get a rise out of people, we all knew that. Especially when he'd been drinking."

"How angry was Shelly about Ryan staying in her house?"

"I don't know. But if I were Shelly, the person I'd kill would be Harv."

Betsy sighed, agreeing with that sentiment. "Tell me more about Ryan."

"He always was a troubled sort of person, but deep down he was full of feelings. I felt enormous compassion for him, and thought I was the only person who really understood him. Which turned out not to be true, of course. I don't know if his problems were so bad because his family protected him from the consequences of his behavior too much when he was young, or because he started drinking long before anyone knew it was a problem with him. I do know he quit drinking the second I threw him out, but he's quit before and he only stayed sober eleven days this time. He told me that night he tried to come home — drunk again — that someone ambushed him with alcohol, though I don't see how that's possible."

"Did he say who did it?"

"He said it was Leona Cunningham."

Betsy retrieved Billie's cell phone number from her list of committee members, and dialed it.

"Hello?" said Billie's harassed-sounding voice a few rings later.

"Billie, it's me, Betsy. I know you're frantically busy, but I really need to talk to you, for just a few minutes. It's about the Ryan murder, and Leona."

Billie asked, "Are you letting the talk going around about her get to you after all?"

"No, of course not! But I'm looking at everyone who had a run-in with Ryan, and that includes Leona." Betsy was sitting in her car in the parking lot behind the small, nondescript brick building that was city hall.

"Doesn't she have an alibi?"

"For most of the time in question, yes. But not all. Do you know what caused Ryan to decide Leona was trying to curse him?"

"Do you have a few minutes?" Billie asked.

Betsy settled back to listen. "Sure. Go ahead."

"Well, about two years ago, Ryan was going through a hard time — again. It was entirely his own fault. He was quarreling with everyone, and people were getting sick of his attitude. Then that incident with the money manager — What was his name? Wainwright, that's it, Adam Wainwright — happened. You know, the fish fell out of the sky on him and he wrecked his car and his vision. I don't know who told Ryan the guy had stolen money from Leona and so maybe she witched the accident on him. He always was very superstitious; it was his way of blaming his bad luck on something besides himself. He absolutely believed that Leona caused Adam's accident with her black magic. He might even have hinted to her that he thought so. I don't know. Or somehow in passing she may have said something to him; you know, on the order of 'Straighten up and fly right.' Whatever, he got the notion that she had her eye on him, and it just grew from there. He'd see her on the street and something bad would happen and he'd remember that she looked at him funny.

"When Leona and I went into business together, we remodeled the Waterfront Café into The Barleywine, and he was one of our first regulars — he liked me well enough, so he'd come in when I was tending bar. Barleywine's beer is higher in alcohol than regular beer — most microbrewery beer is. Ryan only drank beer — he had a notion that as long as he only drank beer, he wasn't an alcoholic. But he was a very ugly drunk and we finally had to ban him from the place. It's my fault he came in that last time, but he promised he wouldn't drink anything but Coke. I tried to keep an eye on him, and Roger swears he didn't order a beer from the bar." Roger, Betsy remembered, was Billie's son.

"He didn't. Joey Mitchell bought it for him."

"That's right, I'd forgotten that."

"To the best of your knowledge, did Leona ever tell Ryan she was going to put a hex on him? Maybe as a joke?"

"No, never. She takes her religion very seriously, and there are some pretty strict

277

rules about that sort of thing."

"Is it possible that Leona slipped Ryan a beer at that meeting? Maybe to celebrate the fire truck's restoration?"

Billie thought for a moment. Betsy could hear her breathing into the phone. "No. Because remember? She was back in the brewery. When she came out to work behind the bar, he was already drunk."

"Yes, that's right. All right. Thanks, Billie."

"Why would Ryan think you were the one who sabotaged his sobriety?"

Betsy was back at The Barleywine, which now had no customers at all.

"I don't know," said Leona. "I didn't serve him anything."

"Not even a Coke?"

"Not even a Coke. I was checking the vessels in the brewery and making sure I had enough malt for when I started the next batch of Don't Be Afraid of the Dark Ale. Roger was working. He tended Ryan's booth, brought him his Cokes. I didn't even realize Ryan was here until he came up to me singing when I was tending bar, and he was drunk by then."

Betsy said, "And Billie only brought him an orange and some sandwiches. Was there alcohol — brandy, for example — in the

278

sandwich fillings? Even a small taste of alcohol can set off a binge in an alcoholic."

"Yes, I know. So does almost everyone, including the people who work here. But no, the sandwich filling was chicken salad I made myself. There was rosemary in it, salt and pepper, mayonnaise, celery. Not even any onion."

"Hmmmmmm."

"Maybe the orange had fermented," said Leona, but that was a jest.

"Very funny," said Betsy. "I want you to talk to me about Billie."

"What can I tell you about her?"

"For example, how angry was she at Ryan for trying to spoil her daughter Cara's chances of getting an appointment to the Naval Academy?"

"I thought she told you about that."

"She did. She says her daughter has finally settled on getting a degree as a veterinary assistant, though that seems kind of a step down from being a naval officer."

"Poor Cara. I don't think she would have made it through Annapolis anyway. Though who knows? She wanted it badly enough. And Billie wanted it for her even more — Cara is Billie's favorite child, though to my mind, Roger is the better bet. Now that Cara's going to be tending sick animals, suddenly that's the best, most prestigious work a young woman can do. Billie not only pays her tuition, she buys her anything she needs for her labs, helps her with her homework, brags about her all the time. She'd take Cara's tests for her, if she could. Fortunately, Cara's not much more spoiled than any kid would be from all the attention. Even better, Roger and Eddie aren't jealous. Maybe it's because they're her brothers, and there's not another daughter to be hurt by the favoritism."

"And what does Cara think of becoming a veterinary assistant?"

"Well, despite Billie's best efforts, she knows it's not quite the same as a commission as a U.S. Navy ensign."

"How angry was Cara at Ryan for shooting down her chances?"

The smile on Leona's face melted and she sighed. "*Damn* angry. In fact, if her alibi wasn't so solid, I'd say you should look hard at her. It's been two years and more, and she still spits firecrackers when someone mentions him to her."

A patron came in about then looking for an early supper, so Betsy thanked Leona and left. She drove back to her shop thoughtfully. Was there a clue lurking somewhere in all she'd learned today?

She parked in the tiny lot behind her shop and came in the back way. As she walked through the little back room into the cross-stitch area, she heard two men's voices. She paused to listen.

One was Godwin, obviously; his light tenor with its manner of emphasizing words was unmistakable. The other man's voice was deeper, and the more she listened, the more she wondered if he was foreign born. There was just the faintest hint of a brogue in the sharpness of his consonants.

So she shouldn't have been as surprised as she was when she came out from between the twin set of box shelves to see it was her new tenant, Connor Sullivan, deep in conference with Godwin over a knitting pattern. After all, his name could hardly have been more Irish.

She stood awhile, looking and listening. The talk was esoteric; the man knew knitting. Betsy suddenly wondered if the beautiful Aran sweater she'd seen him wearing the other day wasn't knit by him. And where she'd thought him rather ordinary looking, now she thought there was something attractive about him. Then she realized it was because he was talking about a subject that really interested him. His hooded eyes were wider open and gleaming, and he was smiling as he gestured at a heap of balls of fingerling wool in a dozen colors, ranging from palest blue to rich maroon.

Godwin had taken up a pair of slender knitting needles and cast on a row of dark green. Now he was working with two colors in a knit two, purl two pattern, switching colors with every switch from knit to purl.

"Before your *purl* stitch," he was saying, "drop the old color and bring the working color *under* the old color and to the *front* of the ribbing *between* the needles, and purl two." His hands moved as he did the two purls. "This is on the right side of the work."

"Hello, Goddy," said Betsy. "What are you teaching Mr. Sullivan to do?"

"Corduroy stitch. He wants to knit a Fair Isle sweater."

Fair Isles, done in the traditional way, have extra-stiff collars and cuffs knit in a heavy ribbing called corduroy.

Fair Isles are colorful, with many rows of small, geometric patterns, knit with fine wool on small-gauge circular needles.

"Have you knit with more than one color before, Mr. Sullivan?" asked Betsy, not wanting him to bite off more than he could chew.

"Yes," said Connor, "but not as many as this. On the other hand, I can do an argyle without looking at a pattern, and I'm looking for something more challenging."

"Well, congratulations, you've found it."

"Have you knit a Fair Isle, Ms. Devonshire?"

"No," admitted Betsy. "I've looked at them and they're gorgeous, but they're complicated and they take a lot of time. Besides, that business of taking a pair of scissors to cut the openings for the sleeves . . . After all that work, to cut in the wrong place . . ." She gave a dramatic shudder. "Too scary!"

He laughed. "A lady as brave as you afraid of a little scissoring? I don't believe it!"

"What makes you think I'm brave?"

"Godwin here has been telling me of your exploits as a detective."

"Goddy!" scolded Betsy.

But the apologetic shrug Godwin offered was entirely synthetic.

"So long as you're here," said Connor, "may I turn over the signed lease on the smaller of the two apartments you have for rent?" His tone had gone from bantering to serious in the taking of a breath.

"Yes, of course," said Betsy, matching his tone. "And thank you for being so prompt. Still plan to move in on the first?"

"Yes, thank you."

"Good." They discussed the terms briefly, then Connor paid for the wool, a book of patterns, and size three circular knitting needles, and left.

Godwin leaned toward Betsy and leered. "He likes you."

"Oh, for heaven's sake, he does not!"

"Oh, but he does. Inside of six months, you'll have that apartment for rent again, because he'll have moved into yours. Mark my words — on affairs of the heart, I am never wrong."

Betsy shook her head at him and burst into laughter.

EIGHTEEN

All Hallows Eve fell on a Saturday that year. The day was cold and blustery, though it didn't rain. The wind would dash in from one direction, quiet briefly, then come dashing in from another direction.

Excelsior was a small town. This Halloween celebration was one of its more ambitious efforts, but still nothing like Minneapolis's big-city Holidazzle parade. On the other hand, virtually everyone in town had played a part in making it a success and they were determined to see it through. They bundled up and turned out for the big party. The littlest contestants wore their costumes over their winter coats, which made some of them hard to identify. The teens braved the cold, even the one dressed as a gladiator with blue knees. Sales of hot cider and coffee were brisk, and people tended to cluster around the barbecues rather than the croquet court. Few complained; after all, this was Minnesota, when within living memory there'd been a gargantuan blizzard one Halloween.

As the short day ended and darkness fell, a quarter moon overhead seemed to be racing through the clouds hurrying by. Temperatures dropped into the lower forties with frost predicted before morning.

Still, the parade units bravely gathered in the big parking lot of Maynard's, a fine restaurant on the shore of Lake Minnetonka just four blocks from downtown.

Their numbers were such that Betsy began to feel claustrophobic — especially when they were crowded around her, shouting questions. She finally resorted to the police whistle Lars had insisted she borrow from him.

"All right, all right!" she shouted. "Listen up! I have here a three-by-five card for the leader of each unit, telling you your place! Any questions you have, ask your leader, and he or she can ask me! Leaders, come here! The rest of you gather with your units and give me some *air!*"

She had to repeat that three times before she had the air she needed, and frosty as it was, it was a relief.

"Now, where is the leader of the Sheriff's Posse?"

"Here!" said a burly man who was probably about six feet tall in his stocking feet but considerably taller in cowboy boots and a pale Stetson. A gold star gleamed and glittered on the breast of his tan uniform jacket.

She handed him his card. "You are leading off. Do you have your flags?" The three leaders of the posse would be carrying an American flag, a state flag, and an MIA flag. There were eight riders in all.

"Yes, ma'am!"

"Any questions?"

"No, ma'am!"

She checked that off on her clipboard.

"Hopkins High School Band!" she called next, and a girl who seemed too young to be in high school, wearing a raspberries-and-cream uniform, came to report that a tuba player and a cornet player were absent but everyone else was in attendance.

"I am sure you can play so well without them that no one will notice," said Betsy hopefully, handing her the band's card. "Next, where are my candy clowns?"

Six people in clown makeup came forward. "We don't have a leader," said one.

"We don' need no steenkin' leader," growled another in what he thought was a Mexican accent. His costume was that of a Mexican peasant revolutionary with more

287

than a hint of skull painted on his scowling face. Thank goodness his rifle was obviously a plastic toy.

Betsy handed the card to the revolutionary. "Well, you have one now. Oh, and I think you, Pancho Villa, should be careful to steer clear of the really little kids, okay? That face is *serious*. And remember, the candy has to last the whole parade, so while I want all of your crew to arrive at the top of Water Street with empty pumpkins, I want you to make it last the whole trip."

"Gotcha," said Pancho, but he handed the card to another clown in the more traditional costume of orange hair, bright red bulbous nose, and outsized, multicolored jumpsuit with a big neck ruffle. On second look, the nose had a stem like an apple and a gummy worm sticking out of it. The sextet walked off, separating as they went toward various units, raising their plastic jack-o'-lanterns in a final salute to one another.

"Thank you! Okay, next, Joey Mitchell!"

Joey stepped up, looking ghastly in whiteface, his torn and ragged yellow rubber fireman's coat streaked with whitewash. He wore a toy fireman's helmet with a flashing red light on top of it. "We're ready to rock and roll," he announced, waving over his shoulder at the shiny red fire truck parked a dozen yards away, its loud engine running a little raggedly. There were four other people already on board, and when they saw him wave, they waved back. They looked as ghostly as he did, except their helmets were real.

"The fellows say we should run the siren the whole time," he said. "Is that okay? It's not very loud."

"Run it full out once a block, otherwise just growl it. And let it run down every so often," Betsy decided. "And if you get complaints that people can't hear the bands, run it only at intersections."

"You bet."

Next was the Indian war party, a group of seven real Dakota braves with their spotted ponies. They had opted for something a bit more sinister in war paint, using a solid black from the top of their foreheads down to the bottom of their noses and then a single stripe of color from the upper lip to the bottom of the chin. They were wearing breech clouts, vests, and moccasins — and goose bumps, as another vagrant breeze rushed across the parking lot and the temperature dropped a couple more degrees. Their ponies were skittish and they were riding bareback.

"Are you all good enough riders to control

your horses?" asked Betsy. "There's going to be loud marching music."

"We've been rehearsing them with an old boom box, and they're all solid with it," said the leader, a strong-looking man in his forties. "The horses just look flashy; they're not really hot."

"Okay," said Betsy, allowing hope to overcome her doubts as she handed him his card.

On the cards, in big, black letters, were three lines. The first was the name of the unit ahead, the second was their name, and the third was the name of the unit coming behind. (The candy clowns' card just said SCATTER.) Betsy hoped the cards were enough to keep everyone in proper order.

"Next, Hot Air Express!" called Betsy, and a very tall, thin man with dark hair and eyes, gray coveralls, and a yellow wool knit hat stepped forward to take his card.

"Don't light that thing off more than twice a block, all right?" ordered Betsy.

"Yes, Ms. Devonshire."

"Next, Roosevelt High School Band!"

The band director himself was there to claim his card. He and more than half the band were African-American; most of the other half was Somali or Hispanic. A lot of their parents were there for support; most of them were in costumes, ranging from Aretha Franklin to Raggedy Ann and Andy. The band had a huge percussion section, and judging by the joyous licks being played in warm-up, they were going to be the highlight of the parade.

"Betsy?" came a woman's voice.

Betsy turned to see Billie, jiggling with cold and excitement, coming up to stand beside her. "Hi, Billie, what brings you over here?"

"Everything else is about all shut down in anticipation of the parade. I wanted to make sure you've got it under control."

"I sure hope so." She checked her Indiglo watch. "Oh, my God, we start in two minutes."

"Your watch is two minutes slow," said Billie. "I'll get the first unit sent off for you." She hurried away.

Betsy shouted, "Costume contest, over here!"

An adult dressed as a wrong-colors Santa approached: he was wearing a green velvet coat and pants with black fur trim, white boots, and a big, black beard. "I told them just the winners, right?" he said to Betsy. He was wearing an enormous blue ribbon on his chest.

"Oh, no! I wanted all the entries!" She

stood on tiptoe and looked out over the milling crowd. There were people in costume winding their way out. Two were already crossing the street.

"Costume contest, come back, come back!" shouted Betsy, between blasts on her whistle. "Come back!" She said to the Santa, "Quick, go catch the fairy princess and the frog! Get all the entrants, as many as you can find. Line them up behind the band with all the drums!"

"Right!" Santa hustled away. No, not Santa — what would you call him? She realized suddenly how clever his costume was. He had picked its colors from the opposite side of the color wheel, green being the opposite of red. So call him Atnas, maybe?

"Now, where's the float?" There was just one float in the parade, put together by the Chamber of Commerce. It featured a sailboat with three ghostly pirates riding in it. The Hopkins band started to play and drowned out Betsy's voice. She blew her whistle, several sharp blasts, and Lars appeared.

"Got a problem? The mayor's here, in case you're wondering." It being a part-time job, Excelsior's mayor had a tendency to forget even important events. He was scheduled to ride in Lars's Stanley Steamer for the parade.

"No, it's the float," Betsy said. "I need it to line up, and I don't even see it."

Lars, who was dressed in early 1930s gentleman's sporting costume — plus fours, white shirt with stand-up collar, broad suspenders, argyle socks, pinch brim hat worn backward — ran off and came back in short order with an elderly woman who looked near tears.

"What's the matter, Myrtle?" asked Betsy.

"The tractor that was supposed to pull the float has a flat tire. And it's one of the big tires, so there's no spare available. The float is already attached to it with chains and some kind of electrical cord, and the man who attached it has gone somewhere, and no one else knows how to undo that. Plus, even if we could get it loose, and find a truck or another tractor, we couldn't fasten it on properly."

"Oh, damn. I mean, darn. No, I mean damn. Then I guess we'll have to make do without a float. Can the ghost pirates walk where the float should be? That'll be where the costume contest people are. Would that be all right? Where's Lars?"

"Right here." His calm voice was such a contrast to the panic Betsy could hear in

293

her own voice, that it served to calm her, too.

"I'll see to it," said Myrtle.

"Thank you. Lars, I'd like you to pull in line behind the costume contest."

"Consider it done," he said and went away.

"Ms. Devonshire?" asked another quiet voice, and Betsy turned back to see a young man holding his shako hat under one arm. "We're the Osseo High School Band. Where's our place in the parade?"

Betsy consulted her clipboard. "You're behind the Stanley Steamer, which is right over there." She handed him his card. "I know it says you're behind the float and ahead of the Stanley, but the float has been scratched and so I've moved Lars and his steam car up into its place. You got that? You're behind the old car and ahead of those men with the folding lawn chairs."

"I got it," he said with a grin as he did a military about-face and marched off.

That left just the Men's Precision Folding Lawn Chair Marching Unit. Their leader wore chinos and a brown pullover, which turned out to be the autumn uniform of the marchers. "Summers, it's tank top, shorts, and sandals," he said, smiling. "Winters it's parka and Sorel boots. But it's funny how few calls we get to perform once the snow flies."

There were thirteen men in the unit, counting the leader, each equipped with an old-fashioned aluminum and nylon-web folding lawn chair. Lining up four abreast, they did a practice maneuver, lifting the folded chairs overhead with one hand, twirling them once, whipping them down, snapping them open to sit down. Lift, twirl, down, open, sit, all in unison. They put their left foot on their right knee with military precision, then stood up, slam-closed the chairs, and began marking time, using the Osseo drummers for rhythm.

Betsy laughed for the first time that evening.

Diddle up, duddle up, doodle up, bam! Off went the Roosevelt band, the costume contest entrants drifting behind them like flotsam in a boat's wake. Lars let loose his Stanley's shrill whistle, and behind him went the Osseo band. The Men's Precision Folding Lawn Chair Marching Unit brought up the rear, its leader calling maneuvers out by number. For better or worse, the parade was complete and moving. Her job was done.

But nervous about it, she set off to follow the lawn chair unit as it paraded very smartly out of the lot and started up Lake Street toward Water Street. There were people on Lake Street, some in costume, waving balloons, jack-o'-lanterns, and those glow sticks that look so pretty in the near dark. There was a smell of taffy apples, popcorn, and hot dogs, and, suddenly, hot and fresh horse manure — and she hadn't arranged for a street sweeper.

The front end of the parade was making the turn onto Water Street, looking smart, when suddenly there was an enormous rushing sound and a burst of orange light. Betsy gasped as an orange flame shot more than two stories up in the air.

It was Hot Air Express, lighting off the burner in its huge wicker basket. Without the balloon, the height and brightness of the flame was frightening.

The crowd screamed — and so did a couple of horses. There was a clatter of hooves, and the sound of human throats whooping amid the shouts and screams.

As suddenly as it had appeared, the flame vanished, leaving blue-green afterimages in Betsy's eyes.

Betsy dashed to the sidewalk and began running toward Water Street. She could see Indian ponies skidding around the corner, their steel-clad hooves sliding, seeking purchase on the street's blacktop surface.

Not hot ponies, were they? Betsy thought furiously.

Just then, the fire truck's rusty siren sounded, and she could see a spectacular black and white pony, about to become calm, shy violently and almost fall before recovering and dashing out of sight.

With her chest aching, Betsy had to stop running. Something struck her in the face and fell to the sidewalk. She stooped to pick it up. It was a piece of paper-wrapped taffy. She looked out into the street and saw the green Santa wave and smile an apology at her. She nearly threw the candy angrily back at him, but caught herself. None of this was his fault. Instead she waved acceptance of his apology. He pulled some lollipops from his plastic pumpkin and sowed them into the crowd, whose members cheered, laughed, and grabbed, begging for more treats. Santa laughed, too, and disappeared around Lars's big antique car.

Betsy stopped under a streetlight and called Billie on her cell. "Did you see the runaways?" she asked when Billie answered. "Is everyone all right?"

NINETEEN

"What a *great* idea!" Billie exclaimed. "But I wish you'd told me about it! Wow, they came running by like a war party on the attack! The kids were yelling and the adults just loved it! They circled the posse a couple of times, but now they're riding back to their place in the parade. Wow, it was just terrific!"

"Um, thank you," said Betsy, deciding she had enough bad news to share already. "We have a little problem, though. I forgot to arrange for a street sweeper to clean up after the horses."

"Oh, cripes, didn't Wee-Wee Willie call you?"

"Who is Wee-Wee Willie?"

"He's a guy with a two-wheeled cart, a shovel, and a big push broom. He follows all the parades around here, even the ones without horses. I gave him your number, and I thought I gave you his."

"I don't remember seeing it, and I know I never heard from him."

"I've got his number in my cell. I'll call him now. He lives just outside of town, so if he hustles, he can get here in time."

"Thanks, Billie."

Betsy cut the connection and hurried up ahead to see if the Dakota warriors were back in their place with their ponies and if anyone had thrown a shoe, sprained an ankle, or worse.

As she trotted from streetlight to streetlight, pressing a hand to the stitch forming in her side, she wondered if the burner going off again would cause another stampede. One rush up the street was exciting; two would be annoying; three would cause complaints from the rest of the participants.

She heard the whistle on Lars's Stanley go off behind her, and the pleased laughter it raised from the crowd. The Osseo High School Band was playing the "Funeral March of the Marionettes" — Betsy wondered how many people knew that was the actual name of the tune best known as the theme song for the old *Alfred Hitchcock Hour.* She wondered what kind of patterns the precision lawn chair marchers could make to that melody.

She caught up to the Hot Air Express

basket on its flat-bed truck as it made the corner. The crowd here was much bigger, and many turned to stare uncomprehendingly at the basket. Betsy was about to signal to the man in the basket not to light off the burner when he reached up and pulled down a gray semicircular lever.

"Whoosh!" went the burner, and a huge gout of orange flame shot skyward. The crowd shouted surprise and approval, except for a small child sitting on his father's shoulders, too close to the flame for comfort. He started to cry.

The Indian ponies reared and one screamed, but the riders knew their stuff and held them in place. In mere seconds, order was restored in their ranks. The leader of the band looked back at the flat-bed truck, saw Betsy, and gave her an angry stare, which, combined with his war paint, made him seem truly terrifying. She signaled at him to approach. Betsy had been a rider many years ago, and she should have remembered how frightened horses were of fire.

He wheeled his horse around and leaned down to ask Betsy, "Can we move back a couple of units?"

Good, they weren't going to go home. "Yes, I was going to suggest that. I'm sorry

I didn't think of it when setting this up. How far back do you need to go?"

"There's a band behind the old car. If we could move in behind them . . ."

"Yes, okay. Tell the band I said it's all right."

"Thanks." He rode back up to gather his fellows and they clattered after him to behind the Osseo High School Band.

They were still moving back down the parade route when, as if celebrating a victory, the basket erupted again, to cheers and whistles. But the horses, having made their own point, merely snorted and danced a little bit.

One of them left a comment of a different sort on the street, and the multihued clown became extravagantly shocked, pointing and gesturing, while the green Santa made a comedy of stepping around it.

An idea that had been waving for Betsy's attention finally got it. The opposite of black was white. The opposite of red was green. The opposite of lavender was yellow-green. The space occupied by a Mitsubishi emblem could also be filled with a witch's hat.

And now she knew the reason for the dream about the galloping oranges. "Screwdrivers on the hoof," she murmured, remembering the hospital corpsman jest from her days in the Navy.

The reason Shelly's blackwork pattern looked familiar was because it resembled Billie's. No, it was the other way around. Shelly hadn't stolen Billie's pattern. Shelly had been working on her far more complex pattern weeks longer than Billie, who only thought she dreamed it. Billie must have seen Shelly's pattern in Shelly's sewing room a couple of weeks ago.

Remembering how careful Shelly was to shield it from other eyes, the only time Billie could have gotten more than a fleeting glimpse of it was when she was in there looking for a place to put her dry ice.

Which must have been in pellet form, because Ryan stepped on one that had dropped, giving the sole of his foot the same kind of mark that had been made on Betsy's palm.

Betsy pulled out her cell phone again and pressed the speed dial button. "Lars?" she said a few seconds later. "We have a problem."

They talked for a while, then she called Billie. "Billie, we have a little problem. Can you meet me on the corner of Second and Water by the bank?" She cut off before Billie could reply, and when her phone began its merry jingle, she just shut it off.

A few minutes later, she was standing on the corner. Her mistake was in not just letting the worried look on her face stay there. Billie, crossing Second Street, saw her expression and started to frown, too, which alarmed Betsy, who tried to change it to a smile, which in turn alarmed Billie.

And when Billie looked around and saw Lars approaching with that cop look on his face — and another cop in uniform beside him — she turned and ran into the crowd.

Lars almost had a hand on her when she ducked out into the street and ran up through the swinging lawn chairs, taking a knock on the shoulder from one and knocking another over. Lars accounted for three more marchers while following her. Betsy ran up the street beside the men; the uniformed officer didn't cross the street, but instead tried a flanking move by running up the same side.

By now the Indian braves were aware of the disturbance. They moved aside to let Billie run through — she was running up the street, not crossing it — but they made yipping sounds at her to show disapproval, and one of them waved a feather-bedecked coup stick at her.

When Billie got among the Osseo Band members, some left off their playing to shout at her. The uniformed cop moved in, at which point Billie grabbed a tuba player and shoved him at the cop, spinning him around some more to block Lars's approach. She let him go and he fell. Lars had to leap high to get over him. Billie ran into the crowd lining the other side of the street.

"Grab her, stop her!" shouted Betsy, daring to run almost under the hooves of the Indian ponies in pursuit.

Then: nothing. Billie was a short woman, dressed like everyone else in jacket and jeans, and she simply vanished into the thick mass of people.

Frantically, Betsy pushed and wriggled her way through the crowd, standing on her tiptoes now and again, looking but seeing no sign of Billie.

A powerful hand grabbed her arm. "Ow!" she shouted, trying to twist away before she saw it was Lars.

"Which way did she go?" he shouted over the noise of the band.

"I don't know. You're tall, you look!"

He obeyed. "I don't see her!" He turned and called, "Mack! Mack! Down to the corner!" and gestured forward.

"We'll never catch her!" lamented Betsy.

"Sure we will. I've called it in, backup is coming, and they'll be watching her house.

Do you know where her car is parked?"

"No."

"Leave your cell phone on. Call me if you see her." He hustled away.

Betsy turned her cell phone back on and started her own search through the crowd. She couldn't move faster than a walk; the crowd seemed a stubborn thing, determined to block her movement. She couldn't hear anything but the bands — and the whoosh of the hot air balloon burner as she passed it, which brought not only illumination but a touch of welcome warmth. She was cold, cold, cold, with fear.

This was her fault. She should have told Lars and let him handle it properly. Or she should have waited until tomorrow and then told Mike Malloy, who could have arrested Billie at her home, quietly, without any fuss.

Instead here she was, pushing her way fruitlessly through a standing crowd, trying to look over shoulders higher than her head for a person who most definitely did not want to be found. The fire truck was making a sound like a gigantic frog with croup, its bell ringing a dirge, its big engine running more raggedly even than when it started out. The riders were making moaning sounds, barely audible over the other noises, and while most of the crowd applauded, some were hooting back or laughing.

If only she could get up on the second floor or even the roof of a building — but everything was closed, locked tight, lights shut off.

The *whoooooshhh!* of the hot air balloon basket's burner was suddenly close — the thing had caught up with her.

Betsy ran out into the street and around to the front of the truck, gesturing at the driver to stop. He did, rolling his window down to peer at her.

The truck was enormous. It had a flatbed big enough to carry a pickup.

"I need to get onto the back of your truck!" she called up to the driver.

Instantly, the man in the passenger seat — he of the gray coveralls and yellow watch cap — hopped out and Betsy ran back around to him. He showed her a square strap of metal near the front end of the flatbed, then formed a stirrup with his two hands. She stepped onto them, put a foot into the metal square as into another stirrup, then stepped up onto the bed of the truck.

The man ran back and got into the cab of the truck and it began to roll.

Betsy rocked around a bit to regain her

306

balance, then she went over to the basket and startled the daylights out of the burner operator by reaching in and tapping him on his arm. His knit cap was, appropriately, orange.

"Hey! What are you doing up here?"

"I'm Betsy Devonshire, and I'm in charge of this parade. It's desperately important that I find someone who is in the crowd. Please let me into the basket, I don't want to call attention to myself."

It was a tall basket, coming more than halfway up to Betsy's chest. The basket actually had a little door in the side, though it opened only halfway down, making a very high sill for Betsy to step over. There was not as much room inside as it seemed from the outside, because there were four large propane tanks buckled into straps along one side. Still, the basket could probably hold four people, in addition to the operator.

Betsy pulled her dark knit hat down over her forehead and nodded at the operator, who reached up and pulled down his semicircular handle, releasing a huge plume of flame.

Betsy was amazed at how much light it gave off, and how well she could see from up in this basket.

She saw Lars, and the uniformed cop —

no, it was a different cop. In fact, it was a female cop. And there was another cop over there. And another one crossing the street.

But she didn't see Billie. The flame went out.

In the next block was a "park" about the size of the flatbed; behind it stood a parking lot that doubled as a farmer's market on Wednesdays during the summer. It took up an entire city lot, and ran from the restored trolley car tracks on the north to the art supply store on the south. The art store's mural — a reproduction of a Claude Monet painting beside a pond of water lilies — was almost invisible in the dim streetlights. But something moved beside it, heading toward the back of the building.

"Light it up!" ordered Betsy. "Now, light it up!"

With a breathy roar, the flame leaped from the burner into the night sky.

And there was Billie, looking over her shoulder, her face pale orange in the fiery light. Then, as the burner cut off, she was gone, as suddenly as she had appeared.

Betsy yelled for Lars, but the Roosevelt Band behind the truck was riffing on its drums and she was sure no one could hear her but the burner's operator.

She opened the little half door of the

basket and fell out, hurting her knees, then staggered to her feet. The crowd cheered and laughed. Reaching, she found her cell phone and punched 911.

"I'm Betsy Devonshire in Excelsior, working with Sergeant Lars Larson of the Excelsior Police Department," she said rapidly when the call was answered. "There is a woman named Billie Leslie, wanted for murder, moving along the north side of Artworks, a store at 345 Water Street, heading for the rear. There are police all over the place looking for her. Tell them!" She cut the connection and pushed the speed dial button to call Lars.

"Lars, I just saw Billie on the north side of the Artworks building. I don't know if she knows I saw her. I'm riding on the flatbed that is carrying the hot air balloon basket."

"Gotcha. Thanks." The connection was broken.

Betsy went to the front of the flatbed and thumped on the roof of the cab with a fist. It slowed to a stop — it wasn't moving very fast anyway — and the passenger got out to help her down. She leaped into his arms, making him stagger back and nearly fall. Betsy made another swift resolution to go on a diet, thanked him profusely but hastily, and hurried off around the back of the truck, ignoring the stares of the Roosevelt High School musicians.

She ran through the handkerchief park, then across the parking lot at an angle designed to bring her to the back of the Artworks building — and collided with Billie, who was coming out of the shadows in her direction.

"Out of my way!" growled Billie, rebounding and starting to circle Betsy.

"Don't run away, Billie!" pleaded Betsy. "The police are everywhere, looking for you. Stay here with me! Give yourself up!" She moved to block Billie's passage.

"You stupid bitch! You think I'm crazy? I'll hurt you if I have to, but I'm not going to wait for the police to arrest me! Move, dammit, *move!*" Billie lunged this way and that, trying to get around Betsy, who half crouched, arms spread, prepared to grab and pull if Billie got within reach.

Which she did, with extreme suddenness. One moment they were both jumping and glaring at each other, the next Betsy was on the rough blacktop of the parking lot, holding on for dear life to one of Billie's ankles.

There was a sound of running feet and the shouting of many voices, male and female: "Stay where you are!" Instantly

310

contradicted by, "Get on the ground!" and "Show me your hands!"

"Oh, Christ!" wept Billie as Betsy let go.

TWENTY

"Leona's alibi was solid. I knew it wasn't her," said Betsy. She was sitting with the Monday Bunch, splendid in a red and lavender silk shirt that matched the surround of her right eye and (though her gray trousers covered them) her empurpled knees.

Present were Phil and Doris, Emily, Alice, Godwin, Bershada, Jill, and Patricia Fairland, back from a vacation in Arizona with her in-laws.

A banging over near the front door gave away the presence of a tenth person, Conner O'Sullivan, busy replacing the broken door to the shop's antique counter.

"Shelly and Harvey were right on the spot. They had opportunity galore," continued Betsy. "Shelly was upset that this drunk was occupying her sewing room at the behest of her boyfriend. But the house belongs to her. The solution was not murder but an invitation to one or both of them to get out.

"Harvey, on the other hand, was my main suspect. He had great opportunity and what I thought was a superior motive. It wasn't until the night of the parade that everything suddenly pointed to Billie."

"Ah," said Phil.

"Yes. Poor Billie, whose adored daughter had her dreams of a prestigious career spoiled by the cruel and careless gossip of a drunken nephew."

"But Billie had an alibi, too," said Doris.

"Not for the whole time. It takes about six hours for a big block of dry ice to evaporate, but it only takes four for pellets, especially if they're scattered. Billie's alibi really wasn't very good. She said herself that getting out of bed wakens her husband — who would ask, 'What time is it?' She could tell him any time she liked."

"How do you know the killer used pellets?" asked Jill.

"Because of this," said Betsy, holding out her hand to display the fading burn mark in the palm. "This happened when I was conducting an experiment with pelleted dry ice and accidentally grabbed one of the pellets. The size and shape of the burn is the same size and shape as the mark on Ryan's foot. Like me, Billie spilled one or more while she was laying them in little piles, distributing them around the room. And Ryan, walking around in his bare feet getting ready for bed, stepped on one."

Godwin said, "I thought it might be Irene. She kept making those strange accusations against Leona . . ." His sentence trailed off, because Betsy had told him about Irene's spying on Leona on the condition that he not share what she told him.

"I think Irene wants to do some sleuthing herself," said Betsy. "She made the beginner's mistake of deciding who the guilty party was and then trying to prove it, rather than just gathering information and letting that reveal the culprit."

Godwin said, "Tell them about the dream of galloping oranges."

"Usually my dreams about cases aren't any help," said Betsy. "Either they're wrong or I don't understand the symbology or I don't realize it's a helpful dream — which was almost what happened this time. I dreamed I saw a whole herd of oranges running on horses' feet, and I picked one up and tried to pry off its tiny horseshoes with a screwdriver." She looked around the table and met only blank stares.

"Back when I was in the Navy, I knew a couple of hospital corpsmen — medical technicians — who told me they used to practice giving injections on oranges, and that someone came up with the idea of filling the syringes with vodka instead of water. They called them screwdrivers on the hoof."

"Yes, and . . . ?" said Bershada in her dry voice.

"That's how Billie sabotaged Ryan's sobriety. She brought him a couple of finger sandwiches and an orange she'd picked up for herself when Roger brought them to the table during a break of the Halloween festival planning committee. Not just any orange but one prepared in advance to be a screwdriver on the hoof. Ryan said someone sabotaged his sobriety that night. He thought it was Leona, and he was sure anything bad that happened to him was her fault."

"Where did Billie get a syringe?" asked Patricia.

"From her daughter Cara, who is studying to be a veterinary tech. Billie helped her with her homework, part of which is learning to give injections — so she had access to a syringe. It's very likely that Cara and her classmates know that trick with vodka, and Cara told Billie about it."

"How did Billie know about using dry ice?" asked Emily.

315

"There have been stories on the Internet, and it was the subject of a crime detection show. The problem is, it has a sharp odor when it's in concentrated form, and I can imagine that people might struggle against the suffocation and wake up. All Ryan had to do was stand up and he'd be out of the fumes, since it fills a room from the bottom up. But Ryan on a binge, and probably as much passed out as asleep, might not wake up. That's why she needed him drunk.

"She took a lot of chances setting this up. If Ryan had sobered up again after getting arrested for drunk driving, if Shelly and Harvey hadn't gone out that night, she couldn't have put this together. She must have felt it was fate working on her side when she drove by Shelly's house with the dry ice on the seat beside her and saw their car was gone.

"But it was while arranging the dry ice that Billie saw the pattern Shelly was working on, and it snuck into her head to appear in a dream."

"Like your galloping oranges," said Godwin.

"It was probably very much something like that," said Patricia. "Stress or fear or anger — any strong emotion — does funny things, makes you notice things in a powerful but sometimes unconscious way." Doubtless Patricia, who had served time in prison for attempted murder, knew about things like that firsthand. But since her would-be victim was Betsy, and Betsy clearly held no grudge, the others felt it wasn't their part to say anything about it, either.

Then Jill spoke up. "Lars told me that the first thing Mike said to Billie when he came to interrogate her was, 'Why did you decide to use pellets instead of block dry ice?' and right there she figured he knew everything about how it happened, and she confessed."

"And all for love of Cara," said Emily.

"Yes," said Betsy. "She loves her daughter more than anything else in this life. Ryan's stories about her, that she was a poacher who cheated her way through high school, made life very difficult for Cara and spoiled her ambition to go to the Naval Academy. Billie hated Ryan for that even more than Cara did."

"I thought Joey Mitchell did it," said Alice quietly.

"He was on my short list," said Betsy with a nod. "His motive was powerful and he didn't have an alibi that covered the whole time the murder might have occurred. But there's a famous Sherlock Holmes story about a dog that didn't bark. And here we had the same thing. Shelly's dog Portia barks at strangers, and Joey has never been in Shelly's house. Portia has a nice loud bark, but Shelly's neighbors never heard a dog barking that Sunday night. Billie's been in that house often; Portia knew her as a friend."

Betsy hoped there was no one else whom Joey hated as much as he hated Ryan, because he had certainly come close to murdering the man who destroyed his career as a firefighter. But Betsy would not tell anyone about the strange confession Joey had made to her. There were enough lives already ruined by tale-bearing.

She hoped this striking lesson about its dangers would at least prune the Excelsior grapevine.

But she doubted it.

WITCHWORK

DESIGNED BY: AMY LAW

Design size: 80w × 80h

Materials needed:
- Kreinik Silk Mori® 8050, 6123, 6127, 8073, 8075 (www.kreinik.com)
- Kreinik Fine #8 Braid™ 5010, 0556 (www.kreinik.com)
- 18-count confederate gray cork linen by Zweigart, or similar fabric (www.zweigart.com)
- #24 tapestry needle, embroidery scissors

Instructions:
Cross-stitch this design centered on your fabric following the color key and chart. Each square on the chart equals one fabric thread, so stitch this design over one thread on your 18-ct linen.

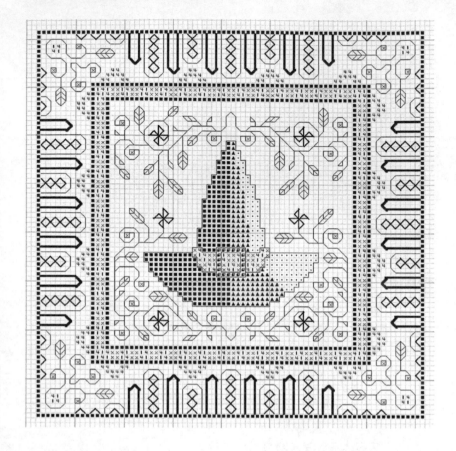

- use two strands of Silk Mori for cross-stitching
- one strand of Braid for cross-stitching
- one strand of Mori or Braid for back-stitching

Kit available for purchase from local needlework shops, or go to www.kreinik .com for information.

- ■ Silk Mori 8050 Black
- × Silk Mori 6123 Lt Dusty Lavender
- I Silk Mori 6127 Vy Dk Dusty Lavender
- · Silk Mori 8073 Lt Charcoal
- ♣ Silk Mori 8075 Md Dk Charcoal
- ⊟ Fine #8 Braid 5010 Knight
- Ч Fine #8 Braid 0556 Fly By Night
- ╱ Backstitch 8050 Mori (hat, vines)
- ╱ Backstitch 5010 #8 Braid (in border)
- ╱ Backstitch 6127 Mori (pinwheels)
- ╱ Backstitch 0556 #8 Braid (border)

ABOUT THE AUTHOR

Monica Ferris is the *USA Today* best-selling author of several mystery series under various pseudonyms. She lives in Minnesota.

We hope you have enjoyed this Large Print book. Other Thorndike, Wheeler, Kennebec, and Chivers Press Large Print books are available at your library or directly from the publishers.

For information about current and upcoming titles, please call or write, without obligation, to:

Publisher
Thorndike Press
295 Kennedy Memorial Drive
Waterville, ME 04901
Tel. (800) 223-1244

or visit our Web site at:

http://gale.cengage.com/thorndike

OR

Chivers Large Print
published by AudioGO Ltd
St James House, The Square
Lower Bristol Road
Bath BA2 3BH
England
Tel. +44(0) 800 136919
email: info@audiogo.co.uk
www.audiogo.co.uk

All our Large Print titles are designed for easy reading, and all our books are made to last.